GIRL IN A BAMBOO CAGE

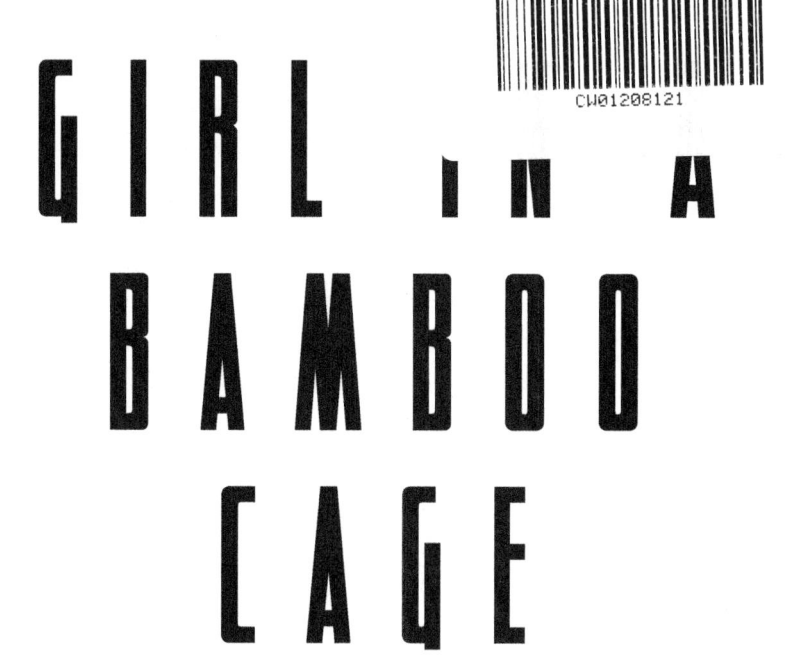

A Jacob Canoe Mystery

Melvin Dill

This is a work of fiction. Names, characters, places and incidents are the products of the author's imagination and are used fictitiously. Any resemblance to actual persons, living or dead, events or locale is coincidental.

No part of this book may be reproduced, scanned or distributed in any printed or electronic form without permission.

Copyright © 2014 Melvin Dill
All rights reserved.

ISBN: 1499218672
ISBN 13: 9781499218671

ONE

Inglewood, California, Feb 1, 1966

The driver turned from the Pacific Coast Highway onto Western Avenue and proceeded north toward Inglewood. It was 1:30 a.m. and traffic was light to moderate with some stretches of no traffic at all. *Take it easy,* she said to herself. She felt anxious and her heart was beating a little faster than usual. *No one knows who I am or where I'm going. Just drive along with the traffic, don't speed or go too slow.* When she neared the intersection at Western and 190th street, the light suddenly turned amber. *Should I go through it or stop?* She slammed on the brake, squealing to an abrupt stop with her front wheels in the crosswalk. She glanced to her left at the car that had stopped next to her. She had to stifle a scream when she saw it was a police car. *Calm down, she thought.* A young uniformed cop was staring at her. She nervously waved at him. He returned the wave and turned back to looking straight ahead.

The traffic light turned green, the cop punched it, hurtling down the street and away from her. She took a deep breath and drove through the intersection.

Ten minutes later she turned off Western and made her way through a series of small streets to the rear of the hospital. A light fog enveloped the hospital and adjacent streets. The glowing street lights were surrounded by an eerie aura. She pulled into the lot and parked in the shadows, turning off her car headlights.

It was an uncommonly cold southern California night so she waited with engine idling and heater on. The inside windshield was beginning to fog up so she turned on the defroster. She had a good view into the rear lobby and east side windows. She could see the guard seated at his desk.

The few cars scattered around the rear lot all belonged to employees. The hospital was typically deserted most nights. There would be two or three nurses per floor. There was no traffic on the residential street behind the hospital. The only hitch to the usual routine would be if an ambulance showed up.

She saw a van coming down the street and ducked down when it turned into the parking lot. The driver pulled to the rear entrance and parked, leaving the truck running at idle. She watched the driver exit the vehicle, walk around to the side and open the sliding door. He removed a package and went in through the doors.

The driver set the package on the night guard's desk and handed a clipboard to the guard. After signing for the package the guard handed it back. They had a few more words of conversation and the driver returned to his truck and drove away.

One

It's only a courier making a delivery. She thought. *Everything is going as planned.* She had had less than a month to make all the arrangements. The birth certificate had arrived at her house two days before. That had been her biggest worry but she was over that hurdle. She had mailed the birth registration form to the county recorder two weeks ago. She had changed the actual birth date and named the baby Jamie, with the same last name as hers. She typed in the father as unknown. With an average 180,000 births in Los Angeles County every year, the forms were rubber stamped and mailed out at breath taking speed.

She checked her watch, it was almost two a.m. She watched the guard turn and look at the clock on the wall behind him. He stood and hitched his belt up under his ample gut. He stretched his arms and yawned, then pulled the seat of his pants from his butt crack and waddled toward the elevator doors. He always went up to the fourth floor and worked his way back down to the first.

If he hustled on his rounds like he was supposed to, it should take him about twenty minutes. He considered himself a ladies man, so he liked to chat up all the nurses he encountered. It was always a half hour or more until he returned to his desk. He was especially enamored of Barbara on the third floor who was too polite to brush him off as fast as the others.

She turned off the motor, got out of her car and headed to the doors. She waited outside, shivering in the damp early morning air, until the guard went into the elevator. Entering, she let the front door close quietly and ran to the stairs, which were to the immediate right of the guard's desk. After going through the stair access door, she climbed up to the second floor as quickly and quietly as she could. The nurses rarely chose the stairs over the elevators so she wasn't concerned about anyone seeing her.

At the top of the stairwell she cracked open the door and peered around the corner. No one was in sight but she could hear voices from the two duty nurses at the desk at the other end of the hall. There was faint music from a radio with the volume set low.

"I'm going to the cafeteria for coffee, want me to bring you anything?" one nurse asked the other.

"Sure, thanks, I'll have a coffee and one of those doughnuts, if there's any left."

"Okay, but it's your funeral, I don't know how you can stomach those things."

"I've built up a resistance."

"I'll be back in a few minutes," the first nurse said, waiting for the elevator.

I'm in luck, the woman thought. *Only the usual two on duty, and now one of them is going to leave for a few minutes.*

From her hiding spot, she heard the elevator bell "Ding," and the door opening. When she heard the door close, she looked around the corner again, *this is my chance,* she thought. She ran across the linoleum floored hall into the open door of a vacant room. She could feel her heart pounding. *Take it easy,* she said to herself.

The nursery was two doors down and now there was only one nurse on the floor. She heard a phone ring and the nurse answered it. She could hear low conversation and then laughter. *It's a personal call,* she thought. She knew the phone cord was not long enough to stretch past the desk into the hall. As long as the nurse stayed on the phone and behind the counter, she couldn't be seen. She padded to the nursery door and went inside with the babies. Standing quietly for a minute, she breathed in the familiar smell of baby talc mingled with antiseptics.

One

She knew there were usually no more than half a dozen newborns in the hospital at any one time. She quickly found the one she was looking for. One of the other babies started fussing, so she picked it up and rocked it in her arms trying to hush it. The baby was getting louder and finally was screaming as loud as her little lungs permitted.

She heard footsteps running down the hall, so she put the baby back and squatted down behind cribs in another row. She was breathing so hard, she was sure the nurse would hear her. The nurse came in and picked up the crying baby and took it into the hall so it wouldn't wake the others. The baby was quiet in a minute so the nurse carried it back in and ran back to the desk and picked up the phone again.

"Are you still there?" she heard the nurse ask.

She waited and then heard loud laughter, and more phone conversation.

It's safe now, she thought. *This is my chance.*

She picked up the baby she came for and wrapped the blanket around her. The baby girl opened her eyes and the woman was sure she saw a little smile, and then the eyes closed. She peeked back down the hall, it was still empty and she could hear low phone talk. As soon as she got to the stairway door, she heard the elevator open. The nurse making the coffee run was back.

She rushed through the door, letting it close silently, and went down the stairs to the first floor. She cautiously looked around the corner into the lobby, it was empty and the guard had not returned. She slipped out through the double doors, took a quick look around, and ran to her car. She got in and put the baby in a bassinet she had placed on the passenger side floor. She took a deep breath, started the car, and then sat for another thirty seconds, looking around the parking lot. *I know I'm doing the right thing. Why should she be adopted by strangers? I can take care of her better than any stranger.* She drove out of the lot onto the street. Her tail-lights vanished in the early morning fog.

The guard had been back at his desk for ten minutes when he thought he heard a scream. He reached over and dialed down the volume on his radio. Then he heard it again. He stood and went to the bottom of the staircase and cocked his head to hear where the commotion was coming from. *It's the second floor,* he thought, *something's going on up there.*

He started to go up the stairs but decided against it, knowing he would be out of breath half way up. He rushed back to his desk and posted the time 2:40 a.m. in his log book. Then he went to the elevator and pressed the second floor button. *Come on, come on,* he said to himself. Finally he heard the familiar "Ding" and the door slid open. He heard his desk phone begin ringing as he stepped into the elevator, then the door closed. Not knowing what to expect and being unarmed, he was tightly gripping his flashlight and was ready to use it as a weapon if necessary. He stepped out of the elevator and looked to his left where all the yelling was coming from. He was momentarily frozen by the spectacle. One nurse was on the floor flopping around and moaning. The other was standing but with her hands over her ears, shaking her head back and forth and emitting a high pitched keening squeal.

What the hell? The guard thought. He slipped the flashlight back into its belt holder. He went to the nurse that was standing and grabbed her shoulders.

"What's going on," he asked. When she didn't answer, he pulled her hands from her head, and shook her, "Shut up and talk to me, what happened?"

One

She finally stopped screaming and was gasping, hyperventilating and trying to speak. She was pointing toward the nursery. Finally, between sobs, she moaned the words, "The baby's gone, she's gone."

"You mean a baby's been kidnapped?"

"Yes, her crib's empty, someone has taken her," the other nurse cried out.

"Show me," the guard said, walking into the nursery.

One nurse followed him into the room and turned the light switch on. She led him to the empty crib.

"That's it, that's where she should be."

The nurse began wailing again, waking one of the babies, which began to cry. They both left the room, turning out the light.

The guard stood in the hall, scratching his head with one hand and his left butt cheek with the other. He walked to the stairway door, opened it and stared in for a few seconds and then closed it. He suddenly had a thought and turned to the nurses.

"Has anyone called the police?" the guard asked.

When neither nurse answered, he shook his head, picked up the desk phone and dialed 911.

Fifteen minutes later the second floor lobby was crowded with both uniformed and plain clothed police. The hospital director, some off duty nurses and another guard had shown up. Personnel from other floors were there. The police started weeding out everyone not considered a witness. Fifteen minutes later all were gone except for the two detectives, the on duty guard and the two nurses.

"Let's interview the nurses first then we'll take the guard."

"Sounds good to me," the other detective said.

"You take a seat over there." The first detective said to the guard, pointing to a row of chairs along a wall.

The guard dutifully went over, selected an armless chair to accommodate his hefty bulk, and plopped down. "I gotta get downstairs to the front desk soon," he grumbled.

"All right, ladies, we're detectives Parker and Reynoso, tell us what happened, one at a time."

They looked at each other, and then one spoke.

"Well, I'm the one that found her missing. I went to check on all the babies and she was gone…and …and her blanket was gone too." She started sobbing again.

"Did either of you leave the desk around the time of the abduction?"

"Only a coffee run to the cafeteria, it's closed after hours but the coffee urn is going all night," one nurse answered.

"Did anything unusual happen tonight?"

Both nurses shook their heads. "No, it was the same old routine," one of them said.

"Okay, thank you. That's all the questions we have for now."

The two nurses returned to their desk and were frantically talking and gesturing to each other.

One of the detectives motioned to the guard. He stood and walked over to them.

"I'm detective Parker, this is detective Reynoso. We won't keep you long."

"When did you first know the baby was missing?" Reynoso asked.

"I hadn't been back from my rounds but a few minutes when I heard a ruckus, and then realized it was coming from upstairs. I came up and they told me a baby was gone from her crib. They pointed it out and, sure enough it was empty."

One

"What did you do then?" Parker asked.

"No one had called 911, so I did."

"Did you notice any suspicious activity tonight, anything out of the ordinary?"

"Not that I can recall."

"Were there any unfamiliar vehicles in the parking lot?"

"Well, I didn't go out there, but from the desk I didn't see anything."

"What did you do after you called 911?"

"Not much, I just waited around for you to show up. Uh, there is one thing, I went to the end of the hall and opened the stairway door."

"Why did you do that?" Reynoso asked.

"I wanted to see if anyone was in there."

"Did you see anything?"

"Nope, nothing there."

"I guess you touched the doorknob to open the door." Parker said.

Realizing his mistake, the guard's face flushed red.

"Uh yeah, I'm sorry, I wasn't thinking."

"All right, that's it for now. We may have more questions later. You may return to your duties." Reynoso said.

The detectives had a conference in the hall after the guard left.

"Well, what do you think?" Parker asked.

"The kidnapper must have used the stairway at the other end of the hall."

"I agree, the elevator opens right here at the desk, and the stairs at this end are in plain view of the desk."

"Yeah, if the kidnapper had taken the elevator, they would have been spotted by the nurses, had to be the stairs." Reynoso said.

"Too bad the idiot guard fumbled with the stairway doorknob. Not much chance of getting prints."

"Whoever took the baby must be familiar with the building."

Parker nodded, agreeing. "That's for sure, or very lucky."

"They also had to know the guard's routine. They must have known how much time they had."

"This definitely smells like an inside job."

"I agree, that's the way we'll put it in the report. Okay, Parker, let's wrap it up and get out of here."

Los Angeles, California, 1971

Jamie was five years old and already knew she was different. She was looking at her image in the mirror. *I don't look different, I look like everyone else.* She watched her mother who was standing behind her.

"Momma, are you like me?"

"No, sweetie, no one's like you," her mother said, pulling the brush through her hair.

"I want to be like everyone else," Jamie said, with a tear running down her cheek.

Her mother laid down the brush, tilted Jamie's head back, and kissed her forehead.

"God made you for a special reason. You should always want to be the way you are."

TWO

Los Angeles, California, 1979, 8 years later.

A woman was sitting at a lunch counter at the L.A. Farmer's Market. The market is a famous meeting place for locals and tourists. The original outdoor market was started in 1934 and has grown ever since. Approximately three million people visit every year and a thousand gallons of coffee are sold daily. The market is always noisy, and the woman at the counter had been trying to ignore a young boy behind her who had been fussing and nagging at his father. She finally turned around when a loud commotion erupted. Suddenly the father yelled at the boy, she heard a slap and the boy was screaming. She was shocked like all the other onlookers.

The father suddenly stopped shouting at the boy, looked around in panic, and asked "Who said that?"

No one answered.

The father put his hands over his ears and started moaning and began yelling.

"Stop, please stop, I won't do it again."

Everyone stepped back watching his antics. He grabbed up the boy, broke through the mob and disappeared in the crowd.

As exciting as the drama was, the woman at the counter was more interested in a teenaged girl who was calmly staring at the man. She watched the girl and an older woman, who was clutching the girl's arm and trying to pull her away.

What's that about? She wondered. Then she did a double take, *wait a minute, I know that woman. Yes, I worked with her. I don't remember her name but she was a nurse at the hospital where the baby was kidnapped. I wonder if that could be the kidnapped girl. She looks about the right age.* The woman grabbed her purse and started after the pair.

"Hey, you've got to pay for your meal," the waitress yelled.

The woman grabbed her check and headed for the cash register. There were six customers in front of her. She looked back and watched the mother and daughter wading into the crowd.

She went to the head of the line, ignoring the angry looks and threw a twenty with the check on the counter.

"This'll cover it, keep the change."

She ran from the restaurant heading the way they went. She spent fifteen minutes backtracking and searching the parking lot. She had lost them, they were gone.

When the phone rang thirty minutes later, her husband's assistant picked it up.

"Mister Harding's office, this is Cecil."

"Let me talk to him, Cecil, it's important."

"It's your wife, Mister Harding, says it's urgent."

He took the phone, "What is it?"

Two

"Do you remember me telling you about the baby girl that was stolen from the hospital several years ago?"

"You mean the kid that could read minds or had some kind of ESP?" He asked, rolling his eyes at Cecil.

"Yes, I saw something extraordinary today when I was having lunch at the market. There was a woman I recognized from the hospital. She had a teen-age girl with her, who looked the right age to be the kidnapped baby. What I saw today convinced me that I was right about her. If we could get our hands on that girl we could make a fortune."

"How could we make a fortune?"

"There's got to be a way if she has psychic powers. I'll let you figure out the details."

"Give me an example."

"Once we find out what she can do, we can take her to Las Vegas on a gambling expedition."

"How are we going to force her to do anything? Why would she help us?"

"I've been thinking about it, we would have to grab her mother. Then the girl would be forced to help us. If she thinks we might hurt her mother, we could control her."

"I don't know. If she has this power that you claim, maybe she could control us. Now you're contemplating kidnapping, it sounds risky, and frankly, a little far-fetched."

"Since when did you become so law abiding? You've broken a few laws in the past."

"Yes, maybe, but kidnapping is a whole different game."

"Her mother is the key. We have to figure a way to separate them. We can promise to let her mother go after she helps us. If the mother was the one that snatched her from the hospital and we let her go later, she's not going to the cops."

"How are we going to find her? She hasn't been found in thirteen years."

"You could hire private detectives, she must live somewhere in the L.A. area."

"Well, I don't know, if the police couldn't find her, how can anyone find her? I'll have to think about it. Tell me what happened at the market today."

She related the events at the market.

"Well, what do you think?" She asked.

"You don't know that the girl had anything to do with his behavior. She was just looking at him like everyone else, including you. Maybe he was just a nut."

"We've got the money to hire an investigator. I'm convinced I'm right."

"Okay, I'll call a local firm I've used before and see what they can dig up, but a lot of years have passed since the child was kidnapped."

THREE

Four months later, Baxter Harding was on a flight from Los Angeles to Wichita, Kansas. He was re-reading the L.A. firm's report regarding the kidnapped girl. They had not found her after an extensive search. Interviewing everyone that was familiar with the case had been fruitless. The police would not release any information, since it was still an open case. The hospital employee information was confidential and would not be provided. The few ex-employees they did find claimed to have no information regarding the child. The investigators concluded that they had exhausted all leads, and that it would be of no value to invest more time and resources looking for the girl.

On an odd note, which appeared to confirm his wife's conclusion about the girl, it seemed that the nurses' taking care of the child felt some special attachment to her. They had constantly argued over taking care of her and were especially distressed when she went missing. The detective agency recommended a firm in Wichita that was noted for success in finding missing persons.

Harding buckled up when he heard a chime and the seatbelt light came on. He had a window seat and looked down to see scattered farm houses, rolling fields of crops and pastures with cattle grazing. Then the city came into view as the airplane banked, preparing to land. He saw two serpentine rivers from the north converging into one near the city center, surrounded by a large green area.

Harding walked from the terminal to the curb and hailed a taxi. He was wearing a light gray suit, white shirt, pin striped tie and polished black shoes. The only luggage he carried was a black briefcase. When the taxi stopped next to him, the driver hustled around to open the rear door.

"May I take that case, sir?"

"No thanks, I'll carry it," he answered, as he got into the cab.

The driver got behind the wheel and tripped the meter.

"Where we going?" The cabbie asked in a nasal Midwest drawl.

"Do you know the Morgan Detective Agency?"

"Yep, I sure do," the cabbie answered, pulling away from the curb.

"That's where we're going," Harding said, rolling the window down.

He settled back in the seat and took a deep breath, "I love this fresh air. It sure beats the L.A. smog."

It was his first trip to Wichita and he admired the broad avenues into town. The streets were lined with trees and grass. There was more greenery than asphalt here which was not the case in Los Angeles, and the traffic moved right along as compared with the constant back-up in L.A.

Thirty minutes later the cabbie pulled to the curb in front of an old three story brick building.

Pointing, the driver said, "There's the front door, the office is upstairs, second floor. Shall I wait for ya?"

"No thank you, I may be a while."

Three

Harding exited the cab, paid the fare and the driver pulled away. He entered a small lobby with a real estate office on one side and a barber shop on the other. A hall extended to the rear of the building with other doors on both sides. Left of center was a wooden staircase. His footsteps echoed off the bare walls as he walked down the hall.

To the right was an elevator, old enough to have been assembled by Elisha Otis, himself. He rode the shaky, noisy elevator to the second floor and exited into a hall. On the wall was a sign saying; "Morgan", with an arrow, pointing down the hall. He found the door, entered and was greeted by an attractive middle-aged woman.

"Hello, I'm Beth," she said. "Do you have an appointment?"

"Yes, I am Baxter Harding."

Beth pushed the intercom button, "Mister Harding is here."

The inner door opened, a giant of a man filled the doorway.

"Come in, Mister Harding, I'm Tom Morgan."

Tom Morgan was born in Wichita in 1921. His father Patrick was only one year old when he and his parents arrived from Ireland. The steamer sailed from Liverpool and landed in New York City in the year 1895. After passing through newly opened Ellis Island, the Morgan family found their way to the Irish enclave in lower Manhattan.

The elder Morgan soon found work on the docks. After beating a few men unmercifully for their insults and taunts regarding his Irish roots, the family settled in. Young Patrick survived as a typical street tough and sporadically attended school. To his parent's pride, he learned to read and write. In 1910, when he was sixteen years old, he lied about his age and joined the NYPD.

Because the police force was over fifty percent Irish lineage, he fit in neatly. In 1918, the year of the influenza pandemic, Patrick was twenty four years old. A tragedy struck when both parents fell sick and died within a month of each other. Having no family left and fed up with the squalor of New York, he decided to take Horace Greely's advice and go west. One week later, with a letter of recommendation in his pocket, he stepped off a train in Wichita, Kansas. He was immediately hired and became a member of the Wichita Police Department.

Two years later Patrick married Hannah Merkel, daughter of German immigrant farmers. In 1921, their son Thomas was born. Five years later they adopted an abandoned orphan boy and named him Joseph.

When Pearl Harbor was bombed December 7, 1941, Tom Morgan joined the United States Marines, where he served in the South Pacific. After the war he returned to Wichita and in December 1945, followed in his father's footsteps and joined the police department. By 1950 he had earned many commendations and was promoted to Chief Homicide Detective. He retired with honors in 1968 and established his private investigation firm. By 1979 he had a long client list and was well known in the Midwest states.

Harding walked across the polished oak floor, noting Morgan's large desk. Sitting on one corner was a shallow basket filled with paperwork. There were five filing cabinets along one wall and two chairs in front of the desk. A vase of fresh cut flowers was sitting on top of the middle cabinet. Probably a touch by the receptionist, Harding thought.

Three

Morgan motioned to a chair in front of the desk. Harding sat and slid a business card across the desk.

That's an expensive suit, Morgan thought.

Morgan spoke first, "Well, Mister Harding, I see by your card, you're an attorney. How can we help you?"

"We would like to hire your services to find a missing girl."

Morgan nodded, "We might be able to do that. How old is the girl?"

"She would be thirteen now, do you mind if I smoke?" Harding asked, eyeing the ashtray.

"No, go ahead," Morgan said.

Harding pulled out a monogrammed case and offered a cigarette to Morgan, which he took. They both tamped down the cigarettes, Morgan on his desk, Harding on his cigarette case. Harding produced a lighter, flicked it open, fired it up and reached over to light Morgan's cigarette. Then he lit his own and blew out a plume of smoke. Morgan slid the brass ashtray between them. It was fashioned from the cut off bottom of a large caliber artillery shell.

"So, is the missing girl here in Wichita?" Morgan asked.

Harding had been eyeing the wall behind Morgan. It was covered with certificates and other memorabilia. A framed shadowbox full of military medals was mounted next to a picture of soldiers. They were posed with rifles, in front of palm trees, with a remote view of water behind them. None of them were smiling. Another picture was of Morgan in police uniform, shaking hands with a civilian, perhaps a city official.

"No, we suspect she's somewhere in the L.A. area." Harding answered.

Morgan wrinkled his brow, took a deep pull on his smoke, then reached over and flicked the ash into the ashtray.

"Why come to us? We could recommend some very fine Los Angeles firms."

"We are familiar with your firm's reputation for finding missing persons. We are willing to pay well."

Morgan stood, walked to the window and slid it up. A breeze of fresh air streamed in. He stared down at the street below, not looking at anything in particular.

He looked back at Harding and smiled. "Beth doesn't like the smell of smoke, and she's the boss in this office."

Jake's wrapping up an assignment now, Tom thought, *this could be a good project for him.*

Returning to his desk, he asked, "How long has the girl been missing?"

"Since she was born, or to be more precise, since she was about a month old, when she was kidnapped from the hospital, so it's been thirteen years."

Morgan paused and shook his head. "That's a very long time to be missing. The trail must be cold by now. I'm sure the police and the F.B.I. have been looking for her all these years."

"Yes, they were looking hard for a couple months. Gradually the case fell off the radar. I'm sure it's still an open case, but there's no real investigative activity. The newspapers even lost interest."

"What's your involvement with the case?" Morgan asked.

"We were hired a few months ago, to find a missing woman, an adult, by her father. He resides in Europe and had not seen or heard from his daughter since 1965. It didn't take much research to find that the daughter died in an automobile accident. She was pregnant at the time and the baby was delivered by cesarean surgery before she died. That baby is the child in question."

Three

Harding paused while Morgan made notes. Morgan stopped writing, looked up and nodded for him to continue.

"An extensive search turned up no relatives and the baby's father was unknown. The child was kidnapped from the hospital before adoption procedures were completed. Now our client wants to find his granddaughter."

"Hmm, an interesting case, we might consider it. Although, this sounds like a tough one considering the time that has passed. I do have an investigator who might be able to find the girl, if she's still alive. I'm sure you realize it'll be expensive to send a man to the west coast."

"What would your fee be?"

"It's a thousand per day, with a minimum of ten days."

"That's a little more than we anticipated, Mister Morgan."

Morgan shrugged, "Some agencies charge less than us and some charge more. Good service doesn't come cheap. Like I said, we can recommend an L.A. firm."

Harding set his briefcase on the desk, opened the snaps, reached in and pulled out a check, which he handed to Morgan.

"All right, you've got a deal, Mister Morgan. This certified check is for fifteen thousand. If you locate the child before the money's gone, you may keep the balance. If you have not found the girl by then, we may issue another check if we feel progress is being made, or if it looks hopeless, we may cancel the investigation."

Morgan pulled open a drawer and dropped the check in. He reached over and they shook hands. *That was easy,* he thought, *maybe too easy.* He pushed the intercom button and Beth came in.

21

"Beth, please draw up a standard contract for Mister Harding, one thousand per day. Give Mister Harding a receipt for fifteen thousand. When Jake checks in, tell him we've got a new assignment for him."

Harding spoke, "We have a suite reserved at the Savoir Regent on Wilshire, and a car will be available for your man. By the way, what's his name?"

"Jacob Canoe," Morgan answered.

"Let us know when Mister Canoe is arriving at LAX, we'll have a car pick him up and take him to his hotel. I'll see him after he gets in and fill him in on any other information we have."

"It'll be a day or two. I'll call when he's on the way."

After signing the contract and getting his receipt, Harding took the elevator down to the main floor. He went to the curb and hailed the first cab to drive by.

"Take me to the airport."

FOUR

Big Stu slid the file across the desk to me. It was a list of arrests and convictions for a miscreant by the name of Homer Scoggins. Description: white male, D.O.B. 6/15/1927, 5-10, 220. Two page rap sheet, a third page consisted of comments by arresting officers. A photo was paper clipped to the file. The picture showed an angry looking bald man.

I scanned the list and noted arrests for assault, petty theft, strong arm robbery, attempted rape, possession of an illegal substance, breaking and entering, resisting arrest, that's where I quit reading. It appeared that Scoggins had been charged with about every crime on the books. I was surprised to read that he had done very little actual jail time. The charges had been dropped many times because the witness didn't show up in court or the victim would not prefer charges.

I softly whistled. "Damn, Stu, this guy is one bad hombre."

"Well, that's why I called you, Jacob. You're not afraid of him are you?"

I looked up and smiled at Stu.

"Don't pull that on me, Big Stu, you know I'll accept the job."

Stu removed the cigar from his mouth, laid it in the ash tray and smiled back at me with yellow teeth. Stu was the owner of Stuart's Bail Bonds. His office was directly across from the Main Street police station. His billboard sign was visible from all five floors of the jail's front windows. It was a very advantageous business location.

"C'mon Jacob, drop the 'big', just call me Stu."

Stu probably tipped the scales at 400 pounds, so he was aptly named.

I kept waving cigar smoke from my breathing space. Finally I stood, walked over, opened the door and snapped the door stop down with my foot. Big Stu had two bad habits that I knew of, smoking and eating.

"What was he charged with this time?" I asked, returning to my seat.

"His most common offense," Stu answered, "Which would be assault and battery."

"With his record, how'd this guy get bail?"

"His wife pleaded for his release, and some liberal judge set the bail at five grand. Funny thing, she had called the cops on him several times for spousal abuse. Now she's begging to get him out. I told her five hundred up front and four back when he showed for his court date. I was surprised when she ponied up the cash. She must have had the money rat-holed or Scoggins would have already blown it on booze and cooze."

"How long's he been gone, Big Stu?"

"Please Jacob, it's just Stu. The absconder has been gone ten days now, I told his old lady she had a week to find him and get his ass into jail and I wouldn't penalize her. Now she's going to forfeit the whole five bills."

Four

Still eyeballing the report, I asked, "How'd you get this rap sheet, isn't this a confidential police report?"

"I've got a source inside, it cost me a sawbuck. Memorize the information, keep the picture. I'm going to destroy the report as soon as you leave."

I read the last page which said to contact Sergeant Buchanan at the WPD for any further information. I jotted down the cop's name and the current address for Scoggins and stuck the photo in my pocket. I tossed the report back to Big Stu.

"Okay, Stu, I'll do it for two hundred."

"Dammit Jacob, you're a bigger thief than some of those criminals in lockup across the street, I'll give you a hundred."

I glanced across the office at an empty desk. "If you don't want to pay me the two bills, send your son, Little Stu, to bring him in. It'll be good experience."

"Now you're trying to needle me, Jacob. You know Junior is merely a pencil pusher. He didn't have the advantage you had when you were young."

"And what advantage would that be, Stu?"

"You grew up on the wrong side of the tracks, so to speak, where you developed the survival instinct and a penchant for violence."

"Now you're trying to flatter me, Stu."

Stu grinned and shrugged, "It was worth a shot."

"Okay Stu, this is the best deal you're going to get, it'll be two hundred if I get him behind bars by 6:00 p.m. today. If it takes longer, I'll drop it twenty five bucks a day."

Stu sighed, "All right, Jacob, but you're not giving me much of a profit margin. I've got a lot of overhead here."

"You'll get over it."

Stu finished filling out the contract, we both signed and he gave me my copy. He lifted his stogie from the ashtray and relit it.

"Thank you, Big Stu, get my cash ready, I'll see you later."

As I went out, I heard him yelling. "Dammit, call me Stu, not Big Stu, and you left the door open."

I flipped him off over my shoulder. I could still hear him laughing when I got into my car. I cranked it over and pulled from the curb into the traffic.

Since the Police station was practically across the street, I drove to the corner, turned left, circled the block and parked in the rear of the station.

The desk sergeant saw me coming, "Hello, Jake," he said.

He laid down his pen and waited for me to state my business.

"Good morning, Harold, is Sergeant Buchanan available?"

He swiveled his chair and studied the duty board mounted on the wall behind him.

"Yeah, he's somewhere in the building, I'll scare him up for you."

He keyed a microphone, "Sergeant Buchanan, please report to the first floor rear desk."

I sat on a bench along the side wall with several other visitors, who were waiting for someone or something. A couple of them looked nervous.

Two minutes later the elevator arrived, the door opened and a plain clothed cop stepped out and looked around.

I stood and asked, "Sergeant Buchanan?"

"Yes, how can I help you?"

"My name is Jacob Canoe and I work for Tom Morgan."

"Oh yeah, Jacob, I've heard of you. How's Tom doing?"

Four

"He's okay."

"I've got to get by to see him. I've known him for years."

"I'm sure he would enjoy that, meanwhile, I wonder if you can give me any info on Homer Scoggins."

Buchanan grimaced, "Yeah, I heard that degenerate has jumped bail, we're not actively looking for him, it's not worth the time or expense. He'll never leave town, so eventually he'll commit a traffic violation or pull some drunken stunt and we'll have him."

"I moonlight for Big Stu, as a chaser. That's with Tom's okay, of course. Stu is holding paper on Scoggins and he didn't show up for his court date. All I have is his home address."

"Well, if you don't find him there, he works sometimes as a bouncer at a titty bar on Oliver. It's called the Rump Room, but he's probably staying away from there too, since he's on the run."

"Does he carry a gun?" I asked.

"I've never caught him with one, but that doesn't mean he won't be armed. I did take a switch blade off him once."

"When I find him, is he going to put up a fight?"

"You can bet on it, he's drunk more often than sober, it'll be better if he's really plastered, but he's still dangerous. Cuff his wrists behind and take leg chains, he's a kicker and a biter."

"Anything else you can tell me about him?"

"He's an ignorant, inbred hillbilly. His mother was fifteen when he was born. There's some question regarding the father. It was possibly one of her brothers or a cousin. Personally I suspect her father. His wife is white but he enjoys the service of young negro prostitutes but not to the exclusion of white ones. He tends to be a salt and pepper switch hitter. A lot of them avoid him, he tends to get rough and slap them around after he gets liquored up."

"All right, Sergeant, thank you."

"Good luck, Jacob."

The cop headed back to the elevator and I went out the back door to the parking lot.

FIVE

That evening, Harding walked out of LAX. The sidewalk was crowded with travelers, shoving their way to get inside the terminal, with others heading for the parking garages or the curb. In addition to the travelers, there were the usual beggars, pickpockets, hookers and other con artists, plying their trades. There was always a Hare Krishna coterie, banging cymbals and asking for donations. Kids lined the curb, watching the skycaps.

If some traveler was foolish enough to hand the skycaps spare change instead of greenbacks, for handling their luggage, the coins were immediately thrown into the street. Of course, this was to embarrass the cheap-skates. The kids scrambled through the traffic for the coins. Realizing their blunder the travelers would usually, with shame, reach for their wallets.

A black Cadillac Sedan De Ville stopped at the curb. A big shouldered man stepped from the passenger side and opened the rear door for Harding.

Harding got in and said to the driver, "Okay, Cecil, let's go to the house."

"How was your trip, Mister Harding?" The driver asked.

"Just fine, Cecil, they're sending Canoe, he'll be here in a day or two."

"I still don't get it, why do you think a Kansas hayseed can find the girl?"

"He has an excellent reputation, I made inquiries and they all say he has the tenacity of a bulldog."

"What if he finds the girl and discovers there is no grandfather? He might decide to play big brother and keep her from us."

"Well, Cecil, then either you or Packy will have to get rid of him."

Big shoulders spoke, "Not me, Mister Harding, I'm not getting rid of anyone." They drove on in silence.

SIX

The address for Homer Scoggins was on the far north side, so I headed that way. When I found the street address, I saw it was the Happy Trails mobile home park. I turned in and drove between two rows of trailers.

Happy Trails is not a nice retirement park for the elderly. It's not a manicured park with green spaces and flower beds. There is no clubhouse with a shuffleboard court or pool tables. Of course, there is no swimming pool. The mobile home park is only a horseshoe shaped drive lined with older rundown single-wide trailers. Small weed covered yards are littered with abandoned appliances and cars on jack stands.

The gravel driveway was crunching under my tires as I idled along looking for the right space number. Kids were staring and chained dogs barked at my unfamiliar vehicle.

A group of children started chasing down the drive behind me, probably hoping for some excitement. I spotted space number eighteen and parked in front. The dirt driveway was empty. If they owned a car, it was gone. Screens were torn or missing, window glass was cracked and one window had a sheet of rain warped cardboard to keep the weather out. I could hear a few window air conditioners whining away. It was breakfast time and the aroma of frying bacon filled the air.

Sidestepping a pool of oil on the driveway, I went up the typical three step trailer porch and knocked on the door. I glanced back over my shoulder and saw the kids elbowing each other for position and watching with expectation. A small boy grinned and waved at me.

"Are you from the police?" the woman asked through the screen door.

"No, I'm a private investigator working for Stuart Bail Bonds."

She spotted the kids, "Get out of here, this is none of your business."

The kids shifted around a little but stood their ground. A little girl about five or six years old gave her the finger. The others giggled at that. The girl, pleased with the reaction, did it again.

The woman, knowing she had lost the battle, glared at the kids, shook her head and muttered. "Damn nosey little brats."

"What do you want with me?" she asked.

"Missus Scoggins, you know why I'm here. I'm looking for your husband."

"Well, he's not here and I have no idea where he is."

"I'm sure you know he didn't show up for his court date. The longer he's gone, the worse it will be for him."

"I never know where he is even when the cops aren't looking for him."

"Missus Scoggins, if you can help me out a little, maybe I can help you."

Six

"Is he driving?" I asked, waving a ten in front of her.

Her eyes widened, "I could use that right now, I'm out of smokes and the bail money cleaned me out."

I tucked the bill under an aluminum support strip on the screen door.

"Yeah, we only got one car and he took it, I have to walk everywhere now."

"Describe the car."

"It's a '65 Dodge, dark blue color, Kansas plate number GGP709."

Her eyes kept shifting back to the ten spot.

"And, what else?"

"Let's see, four door, rust along the kick panels."

"And, what else?"

I waited while she screwed up her face, thinking, hoping desperately for the ten dollars.

"The only other thing I can come up with is; it's got a broken taillight on the driver side. He's too cheap to buy another lens so he taped a piece of red cellophane over it."

"All right Missus Scoggins, thank you."

I walked away leaving her the ten dollar bill. I heard her open the screen door to grab the money.

As I headed for my car the group of kids scattered except for one solemn faced little girl. She followed me to the car, grabbed my sleeve and tugged on it.

When I looked down at her, she whispered to me in a plaintive voice.

"Are you my daddy?"

My eyes stung with empathy for the girl. "No, I'm not, what's your name?" I asked.

33

"My name's Lisa," she said.

She had the saddest eyes. I touched her cheek as I got into my car, "Goodbye, Lisa, I hope you find your daddy."

All the kids were gone as I drove out except for the fatherless child. In my rear view mirror I could see her still standing in the driveway.

I headed south on Broadway, turned left on 21st Street and bounced over the railroad tracks. I rolled up my window and turned on the AC as I passed the stockyards.

My next stop was the Rump Room. It was around noon and already a dozen or so vehicles were in the parking lot. The front door was open and I could hear music as I climbed out of my car. It was a typical low rent slop chute, full of smoke and the stench of stale beer. The floor was littered with cigarette butts and felt sticky to the soles of my shoes.

The day was beginning to heat up and the half dozen ceiling fans were only succeeding in shoving the hot humid air around. Customers were scattered around the room, most were ignoring the two bored looking dancers gyrating on a low stage. The chatter was low except for an occasional outbreak of laughter. I heard the click of billiard balls and saw one man, by himself, practicing on a pool table. He was obviously hoping to sucker someone in for a game of eight-ball. I braced the female bar tender with the photo.

"Yes, I know him, that's Homer, I haven't seen him lately. He works here on and off as a bouncer."

"When did he last work?" I asked.

Six

"I don't know, maybe a month ago. If you can get away with it, please do everyone a favor and shoot the sadistic son of a bitch."

"Okay if I circulate and ask a few patrons if they've seen him around?" She shrugged, "Sure, go for it."

The lighting was dim, which helped mask the features of the vacant eyed, jaded dancers. No one recognized the picture of Scoggins although a few said maybe they'd seen him around, but didn't know him. I finally caught up with the waitress who was scooting around from table to table, delivering mugs and pitchers of beer.

"Oh yeah, that's Scoggins, he's never here unless he's working. He has a liking for colored gash, so you might find him holed up somewhere, trying to change his luck." She winked at me.

"Do you have any idea where he might be hiding out?" I asked, pulling a ten out of my wallet.

Her face lit up at the bill, "I know someone who may know where he is."

She scribbled a phone number on a scrap of paper and handed it to me.

"Don't let anyone else know I gave you this, ask for Tessie, tell her Sparrow said to call."

"Sparrow?"

She grinned and snatched the ten dollar bill, "Yeah, that's me. Tessie might be keeping tabs on his where-a-bouts. He hurt her bad a few months ago, stitches, I heard."

"Thanks, Sparrow, see you around."

"Anytime, handsome, you can find me here most days."

I went to the corner pay phone outside the bar, closed the door and dialed Tessie. I identified myself and told her I was looking for Scoggins. She went berserk at his name. After she calmed, I told her he had skipped bail and I wanted to get him back behind bars. Suddenly I was her best friend.

"He did things to me that I'll never forget. I hope you give him a good ghetto whupping before you take him in. I been carry'n a coiled up bicycle chain in my purse, hope'n to catch him unawares some time."

"Do you know where I can find him?"

"Maybe, him and a couple other white trash hill-billies have a shack up pad over to Central Street. He might be there."

"Do you have the address?" I asked.

"No, but pick me up and I'll show the way."

She gave me her address, *now I'm getting somewhere,* I thought.

Fifteen minutes later I pulled up in front of her place, the door opened and she came running out.

She leaned in the window, "Jake?" she asked.

"Yeah, Tessie, that's me."

She opened the passenger door and scooted in. She was dressed in a mini-skirt and heels, looking like she was ready to go on the stroll.

"Uh, hey Jake, is there any money in this for me? I'm a little short and the rent's due."

"Definitively, Tessie, there'll be something for you when we find his car. I have a description of his ride."

She directed me to a street south of Central where we cruised past a row of run down duplexes.

Six

"Go down this alley, there's a two story in the back. He and his pals use the upstairs unit. He might be holed up in there."

She pointed out the building, and there sat his car, with the tell-tale red cellophane as a pseudo light lens. I parked alongside the building and killed the engine.

Handing her a twenty, I said, "You better scram, Tess, this could get rough."

She exited the passenger side, while I slid out my side and headed for the outside stairs. I went slowly up, stepping lightly. If you run up too fast on these old stairs, the whole house shakes from the vibration. I paused outside the door, noting that the window blinds were closed. I put my ear up to the door and heard sounds of anguish or perhaps love moans.

There was a single knob, no deadbolt lock showing on the outside. The door appeared to be hollow and cheaply constructed instead of a solid security door. I stepped back and charged with my right shoulder. The lock and door jamb exploded in a dozen pieces and the door was hanging open on its hinges.

A young black girl was tied face down and naked on the bed with a couple pillows jacking up her mid-section. When she looked around wide-eyed, I saw masking tape over her mouth. A skinny hop head was on his knees behind her with his pants down around his ankles.

Scoggins was sitting in an old recliner watching the action. When I burst in the door he dropped the can of beer he was sipping on.

I was across the room in four steps and kicked up between the hop head's splayed legs. He screamed in agony and fell on the floor beside the bed.

I watched Scoggins out of the corner of my eye. He was stunned and slow to react. While he was struggling to get out of the chair I gave hop head another kick to the ribs.

"Get out of here right now and I won't kill you," I told him.

I was only interested in Scoggins, I didn't have paper on the freak but I didn't want him behind me while I dealt with Scoggins.

The hop head crawled past me toward the door. He was sobbing and trying to pull up his pants. He stumbled over the sill plate onto the landing. To my surprise I saw Tessie standing there and watched as she put her foot on him and shoved him down the steps out of my line of sight. I could hear him yelling as he tumbled down the stairs.

Scoggins had finally come to his senses. He stood, reeled a little and charged at me. I ducked his roundhouse swing and gut punched him. He dropped to his knees, wheezed and his face turned red.

"Come on Scoggins, you're going to go one way or the other, make it easy on yourself."

He stood, reached into his pocket and came out with brass knuckles. He slipped them on his right fist.

"I'm gonna kill you," he said.

I shook my head, "Big mistake, Scoggins."

He started at me again, only slower this time. He saw I wasn't intimidated by the brass knucks. His eyes were glassy so I knew he was drunk or doped up, but still dangerous.

We circled each other for a few seconds and then he rushed at me again taking another swing. I ducked, he missed and his fist punched through the wall. I broke his nose before he could pull his hand out and he staggered back toward the open door.

Six

I dropped my hands and smiled at him. He didn't have time to figure out why I was smiling before Tessie smashed him over the head with a heavy lamp. His eyes rolled up and he collapsed on the floor. Tessie had gotten her pound of flesh. I had to grab her and hold her from whapping him a few more times. She was cursing and kicking at him.

"Tessie, calm down and let that girl loose. I want to get Scoggins cuffed before he comes around."

After the tape was off her mouth, the girl was sobbing and repeatedly saying, "Thank you, thank you."

By the time I had the leg shackles and handcuffs on Scoggins, he was starting to stir. The girl was now dressed.

"I have to get him out of here and into my backseat." I said.

Standing him upright, I grabbed a dish towel from the counter and wiped a trickle of blood off his face.

Turning to the girl, I asked, "Are you able to walk, or do you need an ambulance?"

"I'll be okay, I'll catch a bus."

"I'll go with her," Tessie said.

They each gave Scoggins a kick in the legs as they walked by. He winced with pain and slurred, "Damn."

He was still groggy, I muscled him down the stairs, one step at a time, and into my car. I waved a beaver tail sap in front of his face.

"Scoggins, if you give me any problems, I'll slap you across the skull with this." He sat timidly and was quiet on the way to the station.

I parked in the back lot at the WPD and led Scoggins up the steps and in the back door.

The desk sergeant smiled, "Well, hello Homer, welcome back."

"He has a warrant for failure to appear, I need a receipt for him. I'm working for Big Stu." I said.

The officer keyed the microphone, "I need a volunteer at the rear desk to escort Mister Homer Scoggins to a cell."

Thirty seconds later I heard footsteps rushing down the halls from both sides. Seconds later the elevator door opened and suddenly we were surrounded by six uniformed cops. I removed the restraints and they hustled Scoggins into the elevator and the door closed. Before the elevator moved, I could hear scuffling and shouts from inside.

"Hmm, he must have slipped and fell," I said.

The desk sergeant smiled, "Yeah, sounds like it, thanks Canoe, here's your paperwork, see you next time."

I circled the block and parked in front of Big Stu's. It was not yet two p.m. so Scoggins was behind bars well before the 6:00 p.m. deadline. Stu owed me two hundred dollars. I had shelled out forty for information, one sixty is not bad for a half day's work.

When I opened the door, I put the stop down to keep it open. Stu laid his cigar in an ashtray and folded his hands on the desk top.

"Don't tell me you've already found him."

Smiling, I shoved the jail house receipt across the desk.

"He's in his cot, nursing a headache. I'll take the money in cash."

"You're a damn crook, Canoe," he said, as he stood up.

Stu went to the giant safe behind his desk and dialed the combination.

"You can try to find someone that works slower," I retorted.

He handed me the bills, "Jacob, you'd really piss me off if I didn't love you like a son."

We shook hands and smiled at each other.

Six

"Thanks for the work, Stu."

"You're welcome, Jacob, see you next time, watch your back."

I drove home and made myself an egg sandwich. After eating, I went down in the cellar, opened my safe and added a hundred to my stash. After doing a few chores, I put on the TV and watched a baseball game. I caught the early news and hit the sack.

SEVEN

The next morning, I called the office at 9:00 a.m.
Beth buzzed Morgan on the intercom, "I've got Jacob on the line."
Morgan picked up the phone, "Good morning, Jake."
"Morning Tom, Beth says you've got a new assignment for me."

"If you can leave this evening, I'll get you booked for the red-eye to Los Angeles. There'll be a layover in Dallas, so you'll arrive in L.A. about nine tomorrow morning. You don't need to come into the office, stay home and pack your bag. Take your ID, but do not take any weapons. You'll be met in L.A. by a driver who'll take you to your hotel. I'll pick you up at your place in about six hours and drive you to the airport."

"L.A. sounds good, what's the job?" I asked.

"Missing girl, it's kind of complicated and I don't have many facts. An attorney by the name of Baxter Harding will fill in the details. This may be a two or three week job, so take all your socks." Morgan smiled at his humor.

"How much time has he paid us for, so far?"

Seven

"Two weeks."

"Okay, boss, California sounds good to me. It'll probably take two weeks to do the job. I may take my swimming trunks along, see you later."

I pulled my only suitcase from the closet and packed it. Then I called my neighbor down the road, and arranged for him to collect my mail until I returned.

I went down into the basement and locked my revolver in the safe. The last thing I had to do was to call Al Riley, the ex-cop who also works for the Morgan Agency. Al has a key to my place and will check it a couple times a week while I'm gone. *Well, that should do it,* I thought.

I brewed a pot of coffee, filled a cup, carried it out to the porch and sat in my cedar Adirondack chair. *All right, Los Angeles, the blue Pacific Ocean, and Hollywood. I'm going to try and squeeze a little leisure time in on this trip.*

My home is an old farmhouse on a county road about forty five minutes from the office. It has a large barn, which I use as a garage and storage, along with other outbuildings. I got the place at auction dirt cheap, and then dumped all my money into making it livable. It was large and roomy but had no utilities when I bought it.

Having sat abandoned for years before it came on the market, the house was in pretty bad shape. The windmill was operable but there was no water piped to the house so I hired contractors to install a pump house with pump, pressure and storage tanks. It was then plumbed to the house. I had a bathroom built and the kitchen sink hand pump was replaced with plumbing and faucets.

There were no sewer lines this far out of town so I had a septic tank installed. A modern cook stove, heating and air conditioning replaced the wood burning appliances. I did all the painting myself. When all was done I had a great house at a fraction of what a new one would cost.

About three p.m. Morgan pulled into the driveway, honked, then got out and opened the trunk. I carried my suitcase out, tossed it in the trunk, slammed the hatch down and got into the passenger seat.

Morgan handed me a wad of greenbacks, "Here's some expense money," he said. "This should be enough but let me know if you run low, I'll wire more."

Forty five minutes later he dropped me off curbside at the Wichita airport.

EIGHT

I had an aisle seat and the first leg to Dallas was okay, but some guy with a weak bladder climbed over my legs every half hour between Dallas and L.A. When my plane arrived at the Airport the following morning, I took the escalator down to the terminal lobby, where there were a half dozen people holding placards with names. One had my name on it.

"Hello, I'm Jacob Canoe. You must be looking for me." I said.

"Welcome to L.A., Mister Canoe, I'm Cecil, how many bags do you have?"

"Hi, Cecil, call me Jake, I've only got one suitcase," we shook hands.

"Give me your claim check, I'll get it."

I looked Cecil over. He was weasel faced with acne scars. His hair was greasy and looked like he was past due for a shampoo. His eyes were shifty and darted back and forth. I had the impression that he spent a lot of time looking back over his shoulder. He probably had done time in the slam somewhere. He wore a cheap black wrinkled suit with dandruff on the lapels and shoulders, which was in contradiction with his oily hair. I took an immediate dislike to him, but what the hell, a client's a client.

I handed him my luggage claim check.

"My suitcase is brown with gray stripes, a bright orange tag on the grip."

When Cecil returned, we hiked across the street and into the parking garage. When we reached the car, Cecil stowed my suitcase in the trunk and opened the rear door for me.

"I'll sit up front with you, if you don't mind. I'm not used to being chauffeured," I said.

Cecil shrugged, "Sure, if you prefer."

Cecil drove out of the airport and took Sepulveda north, where it merged into Jefferson and then Rodeo Road. It was a beautiful warm and sunny day with a few wispy clouds. As we headed north, I could see tall mountains.

"What are those mountains ahead called?" I asked, making conversation.

"Uh, hmm…, I don't know."

What an idiot, I thought, *he lives here and doesn't know the name of the mountain range towering over L.A.*

I had read a tour guide book on the airplane. One of those magazines touting tourist traps and places of interest, so I thought I already knew the answer.

"Could it be the San Gabriel Mountains?" I asked.

"Oh yeah, that sounds right."

I decided not to engage him in more conversation, so I concentrated on our surroundings. This was the first time I had been to L.A. and

Eight

marveled at all the traffic, most of which was speeding. *What's with all the cars?* I thought. *They're bumper to bumper at ten a.m.*

I was trying to acclimate myself by studying all the street names. It didn't work. Cecil made a left on La Cienega and took it to Wilshire Boulevard. At Wilshire he turned left, drove two blocks and pulled into the hotel parking garage.

"That's your car," Cecil said, pointing to a white four door sedan.

Cecil parked, we got out and he handed me a fob with two keys.

"Here are the keys."

"I'm going to need a map to find my way around."

"There's a map book in your room, or I can drive you anywhere you want to go," Cecil answered.

"That's okay, Cecil, I'll drive myself."

We took the elevator up to the sixth floor. "You're already checked in," Cecil said, unlocking the door. He handed the key to me.

It was a small suite, the kitchen equipped with refrigerator, electric two burner cooktop, coffee maker and microwave. A leatherette couch, coffee table, TV and desk made up the living room. A breakfast bar with two stools backed up the kitchen. There was a phone on the desk along with a phone book. A *Thomas Brothers* map book was on the table. I could see a bed down the short hall, an open door in the hall was the bathroom. *Not bad.* I thought.

"I'll go pick up Mister Harding, while you get settled in. We'll be back in a couple hours," Cecil said, as he left.

I emptied my suitcase, hung my clothes in the closet and put my toiletries in the bathroom. I sat on the couch, and put my feet on the coffee table. The room was high enough that the street traffic was muted. The only sound was the AC humming. I nodded off and abruptly woke when I heard knocking at the door.

When I opened the door, Cecil and another man were standing there, both smiling. *This must be Harding,* I thought. I stepped back and beckoned them into the room.

Cecil spoke first, "Mister Harding, this is Jacob Canoe."

"Hello Mister Canoe, your reputation precedes you." Harding said, sticking out his hand.

We shook, "Call me Jake, Mister Harding." I said, deferring to the older man.

I checked out Harding, he was well dressed with a diamond tie pin that could have been real or fake. He wore suspenders to hold his pants up over his gut. He had soft looking hands with manicured nails. He was wearing a diamond pinky ring which also could be real or fake. *Pompous,* I thought.

I sat on a stool at the breakfast bar and waited while Harding sat on the couch. "Jake, we're sure that you're going to do a good job for us."

I opened my Big Chief tablet. "Well, we'll see, fill me in. What exactly am I doing for you?"

"We need you to find a missing girl. She would be thirteen years old now, and was kidnapped from a hospital when she was about a month old."

I stopped writing and looked up from the tablet, "So we have no idea what name she could be living under?" I asked.

"No, the actual birth mother's name was Lucille Krentz. She was in an automobile accident on Christmas Eve, 1965. The mother died from injuries but the child was delivered via cesarean. There were no

Eight

relatives located after an extensive search by authorities and the father was unknown. The child was kidnapped during the night of January 30th, 1966, before she could be put up for adoption."

"What's your interest? Why are you looking for her now?"

"I explained most of it to Mister Morgan."

"He gave me some details, but I want to hear it first hand from you."

"I understand, Jacob, approximately six months ago we were contacted by a man who hired us to locate the where-a-bouts of his daughter, Lucille Krentz, the woman killed in the accident. His ex-wife had been living in this area with his daughter Lucille, but he lost contact with them about fifteen years ago. He had received a letter some years ago, from his ex-wife's brother, stating that the ex-wife was deceased and that his daughter, Lucille, was living on her own in Los Angeles. Lucille Krentz was twenty one years old then. After all that time he wanted to find his daughter."

"Do you have the name and address of the ex-wife's brother?"

Harding seemed surprised by the question, and hesitated, "Uh… no, I don't."

"Can you get the name, and find out if I can contact him?"

"I'll see what I can do."

"Anybody want a beer?" Cecil asked.

"Sure, I'll have one," I answered.

Cecil took two beers from the refrigerator, and handed one to me.

Harding continued. "It didn't take much research to discover the fate of Lucille Krentz, the details of her death were a matter of public record. Our client was distressed, but upon hearing that he has a granddaughter, which he didn't know about, he now wants to find her. We hired a local investigator but he got nowhere. We hope that she's living in the greater L.A. area with whoever kidnapped her."

"So you really don't know where she is?"

"No, but this is where we'll have to start."

"She could be anywhere by now, Mister Harding, maybe another country, but I'll see where the trail takes me."

"Thank you, Jacob, that's all we ask of you."

I paused from writing notes, and asked, "How can I contact the grandfather?"

"I'm sorry, it's confidential. You'll have to go through us. He lives in Europe and wishes to remain anonymous."

This is starting to sound fishy. They're holding back too much information. Why would they think she's in this area if they don't know her name or who took her? In *a week, I'll know more than they do,* I thought.

Cecil lit a cigarette, so I stood, walked over, opened the window, and took a deep breath.

"Confidential huh, what hospital was she born in?" I asked, staring down at the traffic below. The window had horizontal bars on the outside, probably to keep suicidal guests from taking a header to the sidewalk, six floors below.

"Daniel Freeman Hospital, in Inglewood," Harding answered.

"Inglewood?" I asked, turning back to look at him.

"It's a small incorporated city, a few miles southeast of here."

I returned to sit on the stool. I took another swallow of beer, and said, "Okay, let's sum up, we don't know her present name, but we do know when and where she was born, we do know when she was kidnapped, and—that's it?"

Eight

"I'm afraid that's it, Mister Canoe, I know we don't have much information, but we're paying you to make your best effort."

"Okay, I'll get started tomorrow morning."
"What are you going to do first? How are you going to start?" Harding asked.

"Sorry, Mister Harding, our investigative techniques are confidential." I could feel the tension in the room. Cecil bristled, which for some reason pleased me.

They both stood, Harding smiled, "Thank you, Jake, please keep us apprised of your progress."

After they left, I took a shower, turned the AC down and stretched out for a nap. I hadn't slept well on the plane, and wanted to be fresh for tomorrow. It didn't work. I was restless and finally got up and took the elevator down to the lobby.

"Hello, I'm Jake Canoe from room 615," I said to the desk clerk.

"Good afternoon, Mister Canoe, I'm Jeff, how can I be of assistance?"

"Is there a library near here?"

"Sure, it's a ten or fifteen minute drive. I'll sketch you a map."

"I need to do some research, what newspapers cover the Inglewood area?"

"Well, let's see, the two L.A. papers, and the Torrance Daily Breeze."

"Is there a good place to get something to eat around here?"

"The Country Kitchen, It's a block down the street."

"Do you have a safe available for guests?"

"Yes, back here," the clerk said motioning me to follow.

We went into a small room behind the desk. A bank of keyed doors was mounted into the back wall.

"Do you have an envelope?" I asked.

I left a thousand dollars in my wallet and put the balance in the envelope. The clerk locked the door and handed the key to me.

I handed the clerk a twenty, and said, "Jeff, if anyone asks about me, where I am or where I went, you don't know anything. Got it?"

"I got it, Mister Canoe."

"I'm going to take a walk and grab something to eat, see you later." I said, going out through the front doors.

By the time I was halfway to the corner I had two pan handlers hit me up. I shook my head no at both. When I saw a third approaching I knew what was coming, so I held up my hand, palm out. The bum got the message and veered off without a word.

When I reached the Country Kitchen I went in and ordered the twenty four hour special, eggs, bacon, hash browns and toast along with coffee. Listening to conversations from other tables while I ate was not unlike anything I would hear in Kansas. Some couples were quietly arguing. Others were sitting hip to hip on the same side of the table, smiling and whispering to each other. Families with children were talking about soccer games and going to the movies. Los Angeles, I decided, was like any other city, only much larger. After I finished eating, the waitress hauled off the dishes and topped off my coffee. Fifteen minutes later, I headed back to my room.

That evening I watched the last three innings of a baseball game between The L.A. Dodgers and the Giants. Then I changed channels to catch the local news.

SPECIAL REPORT: The banner across the top of the screen read. It took me a few seconds to see what was going on. The camera shot was obviously from a helicopter. As usual cars were moving along the freeway, but the camera was focused on one in particular. It was a dark

Eight

red pickup truck careening from one lane to another, cutting off other vehicles. It would sometimes briefly dart into the break-down lane on the right side, and then pull back in front of another driver forcing him to hit his brakes. A reporter was excitably describing the action. About ten black and whites were pacing him, trying to catch up. Suddenly he over corrected and the truck rolled on its side sliding into the center divider. To my amazement the driver climbed out his window and took off running along the divider. Now cops were chasing him on foot and a dog was on his heels. It was all over when he flopped and spread his hands. *Wow*, I thought, *I have never seen anything like that in Wichita. Once in a while a cow will get on the road, but it wouldn't be televised.*

I turned off the TV and went to bed. It was a restless night, a dream kept drifting in and out of my mind. All I could picture was the little girl from the trailer park asking me if I was her father. I couldn't remember her name in the dream. When I woke I immediately remembered her name, it was Lisa.

NINE

The next morning I rode the elevator down to the garage, found the car provided by Harding and drove back to the restaurant.

After breakfast, I studied my map book and compared it with the map drawn by Jeff, the clerk. Fifteen minutes later I parked and took the steps up to the library doors. I went to the information desk.

"Hi," I said, flashing my best smile at the young woman behind the desk.

She returned the smile, "How may I help you?"

"Do you have older newspapers available for research?"

"Sure, what year, and which newspapers do you need?" she asked.

"From Christmas day 1965, through February 1966, the Torrance Daily Breeze and both the L.A. papers," I answered.

"Those are on microfiche reels, have a seat at that table over there," she said, pointing. "I'll bring them over and show you how to use the reader."

Five minutes later she brought the reels over.

Nine

"Are you a writer or student?" She asked, looking at my note pad.

"Neither, I'm a private investigator." I gave her a business card.

"You're a long way from home," she said, reading my card.

"I go where the bad guys are."

She leaned over me and loaded a reel in the reader. After she spent a minute instructing me how to operate it, I said, "I think I get it."

She smiled, "I'll be at the desk if you need any help."

After she walked away, I took a deep breath and got to work. I began with Christmas day. The Torrance newspaper had a brief article describing the accident and reported that the victim, Lucille Krentz, did not survive the accident, but her unborn child, a girl, was saved. I couldn't find anything regarding the accident in the L.A. papers. The story must not have been sensational enough for the big papers. Krentz had taken a taxi from her room on Imperial Highway at approximately 10:00 p.m. The destination is unknown. It was fifteen minutes later when the cab was broad sided.

A drunk driver had run a red light at Imperial Highway and Hawthorne Boulevard. The taxi driver was killed instantly. An ambulance arrived shortly after and the passenger was transported to the nearest emergency room. The drunk stumbled away from the scene uninjured and was subsequently arrested for vehicular homicide.

Lucille Krentz was taken to the Daniel Freeman Hospital, where she died four hours later. The doctors were able to save her baby which was born approximately three weeks premature. Using identification, found on the victim, the police went to her motel room, which she rented on a month to month basis. The clerk was unable to provide any information about her, only that she paid her rent, and kept to herself. He had never seen any visitors.

After searching her room, the police found no correspondence leading to any family or friends. Paycheck stubs led them to a diner a block away, where she worked as a waitress. Her co-workers knew nothing of her personal life, but all said that she was well liked and friendly. They knew she was pregnant but didn't know who the father was.

The police found receipts from an obstetrician's office located in the city of Hawthorne. The doctor gladly shared his records with the police, but there was no mention of the baby's father's name. The doctor said that she refused to reveal the father's name.

Not much information so far, I thought. Then I moved on to February 2, 1966. The day after the baby was taken. The kidnapping of a baby from a hospital was front page news in all the newspapers.

The two on duty nurses, Emma Thomas and Roselda Flores, were questioned and both stated that the child was there at 2:00 a.m., but gone at 2:40 a.m. The police also interviewed all the nurses that were not on duty that night, but had contact with the baby on other shifts. The other nurses were not named.

The OB department head, doctor Stefan Huros, was also interviewed. He was not there that night and was as puzzled as everyone else about the abduction. The security guard for the night was questioned but stated that he saw nothing. All newspapers had the same basic information, probably from a press release by the police.

On an interesting note, it was reported that many of the nurses had an extreme reaction to the kidnapping. Some of them were hysterical, crying and sobbing uncontrollably. It was concluded by the police that their stress was caused because they had bonded with the baby during the month they took care of her.

Nine

The abduction continued to be headline news for a few days, and then was relegated to the back pages. The police stated that they were vigorously pursuing any and all leads and requested help from the public about the victim. Newspaper articles were increasingly briefer until they disappeared completely in three weeks. I assume that in crime ridden L.A., new horrors occurred daily and older crimes were soon forgotten.

Well, I've got the names of two nurses and a doctor, not much, but it's a start. I closed my note book, stood and stretched to get the kinks out from sitting in a wooden chair for an hour.

I returned the reels to the front desk and thanked the girl for her help. I stepped out the library and put on my sunglasses. The sun was blindingly bright after being in the library. It was only 1:00 p.m. so I decided to head over to the hospital. I checked the map book for the best route and took off for Inglewood.

I was a little uncomfortable driving in an unfamiliar city so I took my time and made sure I broke no laws. Of course I was honked at and received the one finger salute from many of my fellow drivers. They knew where they were going and didn't want responsible drivers slowing them down. Enduring the insults, I fought the traffic east on La Cienega Boulevard, south to Manchester than east to Prairie and south to the Daniel Freeman hospital.

TEN

"Cecil picked up the phone. "It's Packy, Mister Harding."
Harding took the phone, "Yes, Packy, what do you have to report?"

"Well, he ate, and then drove down the street a little way and went into a big building. As soon as he went inside, I followed him up the steps. It was a library so I was a little nervous about going in. I never been in one of those places before, and didn't know what it was going to be like in there."

"All right, Packy, did you go in or not?"

"Well, yeah, I finally did, I took a book off a shelf and pretended to read it while I watched him. Nobody paid any attention to me."

"I don't care what you did, tell me what he did."

"He was talking to some girl at a desk, they were swapping smiles, he'll probably be porking her before the week is out."

"Packy, please stay on track, what did he do?"

"He spent an hour looking at some reels on a machine. I couldn't tell what it was. It looked like some kind of TV screen. All the time

Ten

he kept writing in a note pad. Then he took the reels back to the girl and left.

"Okay, and then what?"

"When he left I followed him and he drove to a hospital. I'm calling from a phone booth outside the main door. I watched him from outside. He got into an elevator and went upstairs. I'll wait to see where he goes from here."

"Is it the Daniel Freeman Hospital in Inglewood?"

"Yeah, it is, boss."

"All right, Packy, good work, stick with him. Let me know everything he does."

Packy went through the doors and sat down in the lobby. The receptionist behind the desk looked at him.

"I'm just waiting for someone." He said.

I'm learning, Jamie thought. She had it figured out now. She couldn't read anyone's thoughts and as far as she knew, no one could read hers if she didn't want them to. At first, if she really concentrated on one person by looking into their eyes, she could tell by their reaction that they could sense what she was thinking. She had read somewhere that the eyes were the window to the soul, and maybe that was true. Her challenge was to not give herself away. She had to be selective regarding her actions and the person she was contacting.

Over time she realized that she could just stare at their head and do the same thing. The sensation she felt, was that, she was squeezing or compressing her brain and the recipient would hear the silent message.

She was learning to control the thought and let it slowly and quietly creep into their sub-conscience. Her first experiments were almost disastrous, causing panic or fear in the other person. Now she had refined it to a quiet whisper. *Yes, she had learned.*

ELEVEN

After parking, I entered the hospital and paused to read a bronze plaque on the lobby wall. It was a mini history regarding the hospital. The land was donated by the Freeman family to the Carondelet Order. Hospital construction was started in 1954. Daniel Freeman had been the original owner of the Centinela Valley Ranch which was eventually sub-divided. He was also one of the original founders of the city of Inglewood. The hospital was dedicated to and named for him.

A lot of other visitors were streaming into the hospital. I bypassed the front desk and went directly to the elevators. I scanned the wall index for the obstetric ward, and then rode up to the second floor with four other visitors. All the others went immediately to the left down a hall, and joined other visitors staring through large windows at the newborn babies. I headed for the reception desk.

When I approached the counter, the nurse smiled and raised her eyebrows in an inquiring manner.

"Is Doctor Stefan Huros available for a few minutes?"

"He no longer works on this floor, his office is on the fourth floor."

"Do you think I'll be able to see him?"

"Well, you can try. Check at the desk up there."

I took the elevator to the fourth floor, it opened into another lobby. A stern-faced woman sat at the front desk.

"Hello," I said, "Would it be possible to see Doctor Huros?"

"He's very busy, do you have an appointment?"

"No, I only need a few minutes."

"What's the nature of your business?"

Great, I thought, *she takes her job a little too seriously.*

I showed my P.I. badge to her, "I'm investigator Canoe. It's about a case I'm looking into."

She started to lean forward to take a closer look at the badge when a door behind her opened. We both turned and looked at the tall man who entered. He had an amazing shock of white hair, with a goatee and mustache.

"Doctor Huros," she said, "This is investigator Canoe, he'd like a few minutes."

I breathed a silent sigh of relief. *That was a close call,* I thought, *she didn't get a good look at my badge.*

The doctor paused, smiled, waved me into his office, and spoke, "I've got a few minutes, come on in, I suppose this is about the kidnapped baby."

"Yes, it is, how did you know?" I asked, as I stepped into the office. He followed me in and closed the door behind us.

Eleven

"It's always about the baby. Either the police, newspaper or television reporters are still seeking answers. You're the first one to be around for quite a while."

"Thank you Doctor. I appreciate your time and I'll try to be brief."

"Have a seat," he said, motioning to a chair.

"How can I help you, Mister Canoe?"

"Please call me Jake. I have the names of the two nurses on duty the night of the abduction, Emma Thomas and Roselda Flores. Could you give me the names of any nurses that tended to the child on other shifts?"

"Well, not off hand, I've forgotten the names over the years. I'll get the file regarding the mother and child. We'll see what's in there."

The doctor went to a file cabinet. After thumbing through a drawer he pulled out a manila folder and returned to his desk. After leafing through the file, he said, "I see that Gladys Crain was on OB duty the night the baby was delivered, but not the night of the abduction. I remember her as a nurse that alternated shifts. You can add her to your list."

"What about the security guard?" I asked.

"He died of a heart attack about six years ago."

"Do you have anything that would identify the baby, such as a footprint?"

"Not anymore, the file on that disappeared along with the baby."

I sat back with that information. "So whoever took the child had to be a hospital employee. An outsider could have taken the baby but wouldn't have access to records."

"I agree, why do the police have renewed interest in the case?"

"Doctor, I'm sorry, you misunderstand. I'm a private investigator, not a cop."

The doctor frowned and looked irritated. "May I see your ID? I would like to know who I'm talking to."

I showed him my identification, saying, "Jacob Canoe actually is my name. The grandfather of the abducted child has surfaced and is looking for the child. I've been hired to see what I can turn up."

"If the police or FBI couldn't find her thirteen years ago, why do you think you can find her now?"

"They've quit looking a long time ago, and the kidnapper may have made a mistake after all these years. A law firm has engaged me to investigate. I can devote a lot more time than the police can."

"She may not even be alive."

"Well, yeah, I know anything could have happened the last thirteen years."

"That's true, but not exactly what I'm talking about, there's another reason that she may not be alive."

The doctor returned to the file cabinet and removed a folder. He took out what appeared to be an X-ray. He went to a frame on the wall and clipped on the X-ray. He walked to the window, pulled the shade, and returned to the x-ray where he flipped a switch to backlight it.

"Take a look at this, Jake." He motioned me over.

I stood, walked over to the doctor, and stared at the X-ray.

"What am I supposed to see?"

"See this small dark spot," the doctor said, pointing at the X-ray.

"Yeah, what is it, Doctor?"

"It's a growth between the pons and hippocampus. We kept an eye on it and there was no increase in size while she was here. The child was alert and reactive to outside stimuli, in all, a healthy and thriving baby."

"But you're saying it's possible that something could have happened to her since then?"

"These things are a mystery, it could stay the same size her whole life and never be a problem or it could begin to grow and be a big problem."

"Would it be possible to see employee files for names of other nurses that had contact with the baby?"

"Not without a court order and I doubt you're going to get that. Old records are filed away and in storage."

"That's what I figured, one last question, doctor. What was going on with the nurses getting hysterical when the baby was kidnapped?"

"I'm not sure, it was the strangest reaction. One would think it was their child instead of only another patient."

"Yeah, Doctor, that does sound strange."

"Okay, Jake, that's all the time I have, I'm sorry but I have a meeting, good luck in your search."

The doctor stood, walked over and opened the door for me.

I rode the elevator down to the main lobby and went into the waiting room, where I sat in a chair. *Let's see now,* I thought, *I've got three names, there must be a way I can get others.*

I sat for about fifteen minutes, wondering what my next move would be. I watched an elderly man in coveralls get off the elevator and start walking down a hall. From my vantage point, I saw the man unhook a big ring of keys from his belt and select one to unlock a door.

The man went in and came out thirty seconds later rolling a cart which seemed to carry cleaning supplies. I determined that he was a janitor or worked in housekeeping. He looked old and tired, *I bet he's worked here for years,* I thought, *he might be the one I'm looking for.* The man re-locked the door and slowly started rolling the cart down the hall. I stood to follow him.

Cecil answered the phone, "It's Packy again, Mister Harding." He handed the phone to Harding.

"Hello Packy," Harding said.

"Mister Harding, he's still in the hospital. He went up in the elevator and was gone for about a half hour. When he came down he sat in the lobby for a long time and then got up and went down a hall where I couldn't see him. He might spot me if I go down there, what should I do?"

"Just wait where you are, do the best you can to see what he does and keep me informed. Follow him when he leaves, don't let him see you."

"There are a lot of people here so he don't know I'm watching him. I'm calling from the phone booth. I'll let you know where he goes next."

"Okay Packy, just be smart."

I caught up with the custodian. The hall was deserted except for the two of us.

"Sir, could I have a minute?"

The man stopped and turned back to see what I wanted.

"Whatcha need?" he asked.

"Have you worked here for a long time?"

He looked me up and down before answering.

"Yeah, I've worked here about eighteen years. Who's asking?"

"My name is Jake Canoe."

I showed him my P.I. badge and identification.

He squinted at the badge and looked up at me.

"Okay, how can I help?"

"Were you working here thirteen years ago when the baby kidnapping happened?"

"I sure was, but not the night when it happened, I only work days."

"I have some questions about your recollections of the event. If you would meet me after you get off work, I'm willing to pay you well."

"What kind of money are we talking about? Good money? Make it worth my time."

"I'll pay cash, as much as you make in one week, for a half hours talk."

When the old man looked around, making sure no one was within earshot, I knew I had him.

"Sounds good, I get off early today, it'll be about thirty minutes, where do you wanna meet?"

"How about that Bob's Big Boy I passed down the street, I'll buy you dinner."

"You got a deal, Jake, my name's Ben."

I headed back down the hall to leave the hospital. He went the other way, pushing the cart in front of him.

When I got to the restaurant, I was led to a booth by the hostess. The waitress showed up a minute later.

"Can I get you something to drink, Hon?" she asked.

"Coffee for now, I'm waiting for someone, we'll order food later."

I was starting my second cup when I spotted an old red pickup pull in and park outside the window. I watched as Ben slowly extricated himself from the truck. He came in, saw me, walked over and plopped down with a deep sigh. It seems that the lowest paid workers are always the ones doing the hardest work.

The waitress returned, poured a coffee for Ben and we ordered our meals.

"Cheese burger and onion rings for me." I said.

Ben nodded at the waitress, "I'll have the same."

"Tell me, Ben, do you have a family?" I asked.

"Just me and the wife, the kids are grown and moved out."

"How much do you make a week, Ben?"

"Not enough, that's for sure, about one eighty, that's after deductions."

"Here's two hundred," I said, sliding the bills to him.

Ben's eyes widened, "I don't know what I can tell you to earn this much money."

I showed Ben the three names on my list, "Are there any other nurses that you can remember, that worked in the O.B. ward at the time of the kidnapping?"

Ben studied the list, "Yeah, there was Mildred Lerch."

"Spell her last name." I added her name to the list after Ben spelled it out.

"Did you suspect anyone, or did anyone react to the kidnapping in a way that didn't seem quite right?"

"Not that I can think of offhand. Of course it was pretty shocking news to everyone. A baby don't get kidnapped that often, especially from a hospital."

"Do you know anything about the nurses' reaction to the kidnapping, about how they went hysterical?"

"Oh yeah, I forgot about that. Some of them went absolutely nuts when they heard about it. I guess they were really attached to the kid. Back before she was taken I remember when one of the nurses came in an hour early. The gal she was relieving got madder'n hell and was saying that nobody was going to steal her time with the baby."

I watched him shake his head and smile with the memory.

"It was the funniest damn thing I ever saw. Nobody ever relieved me early and never will."

I decided to go ahead and offer the proposition. All he can do is to refuse me. He had already taken money so odds were that he'd be happy to receive more.

"Ben, do you know where they keep all the records, you know, old employee files?"

"Sure, they've got a big room down in the basement. They call it the archives."

"Do you have a key to that room?" I asked.

He set his burger down and took a sip of coffee.

"Now wait a minute, Jake, I hope you're not thinking what I think you're thinking."

"I need to get in there for a half hour, I won't take anything, just snap a few pictures. Remember Ben, it's for a good cause. I'm trying to find the baby. I'm willing to pay big money. While we're eating think about a figure."

We both resumed eating, I didn't say any more. The fact that he didn't say no was a good sign. I could see he was working it around in his head. *He's going to go for it.* I thought. *I can see it in his eyes.*

"We'd have to be careful. I wouldn't want to lose my job." He said.

I've got him, I thought.

Ben paused eating and wiped his mouth with a napkin. "There just might be a way we can pull it off. I'll get you a uniform and a blank ID badge. You can't be wandering around without ID, even with me. You'll have to have a picture taken to put in the badge, here, see mine."

The badge was about 3x5 inches, with a 2x3 picture. His name was typed in under the photo. It was pinned on his shirt.

"How much money are you thinking, Ben?"

"Well, how about… uh," he hesitated. We were staring intently at each other. I knew what he was thinking; *how high can I go without blowing the deal?*

"Three hundred?" He finally said with hopeful uncertainty.

"I was thinking four hundred, Ben."

I knew that would cinch the deal.

"Oh yeah, I'll take it, you got a deal, we can make this work."

He was beaming with satisfaction at his good luck. He finished off his onion rings, sat back and folded his hands on the table.

"Okay, Jake, when are we going to go at it?"

"I want to move on it as fast as possible."

"All right Jake," he said, "Here's the way we'll do it. I'll meet you here in the parking lot tomorrow after I get off. I'll have a uniform and the blank name badge. See my red truck out there, I'll be driving that."

I nodded, "I'll be here."

"Make it about four to four thirty."

"That'll work." I said.

He smiled, "That four hundred will sure come in handy."

After Ben left I put a tip on the table, paid the check and headed to my car. It took me almost an hour to get back to my room. I opened a bottle of beer, took out my notes and studied them.

I've got five names, consisting of four nurses and Doctor Huros. I've already interviewed Huros. Once I get into those files, I hope to have more information on the others. I took the phone book from the desk. *I might as well start with the most obvious source.*

TWELVE

When the phone rang, Harding answered, "Hello, this is Baxter Harding."

"Mister Harding, this is Packy."

"Yes, Packy, what do you have?"

"Well, I can't figure out this guy, when he finally comes out of the hospital, he goes down the street to a restaurant and he's just sitting there for a while. Then this old guy comes in and sits with him, they order meals and they're eating and talking for an hour."

"Do you have any idea who the other man was?"

"No, I never saw him before. When they got done eating, they both left. The old man went one way, in an old red truck, and Canoe the other. I followed Canoe back to his room, and it looks like he's in for the night."

"All right, Packy, thank you, continue surveillance tomorrow."

Twelve

I started down the list, checking it against the phone directory. Emma Thomas, not listed, Roselda Flores, also not listed, Gladys Crain, ditto. I had no luck until I got to the fourth name, then, bingo. There was a Mildred Lerch listed as living in Gardena. I jotted down the address and phone number. *It may not be the same person,* I thought, *in a city this size there will definitely be more than one person with the same name.*

I dialed the number, a woman tentatively answered, "Hello."

"Hello, my name is Jacob Canoe, are you Missus Lerch?"

"That's me, whatever you're selling, I don't want any."

There was an irritating clicking noise on the phone. "I'm not selling anything, Missus Lerch. I'm investigating a kidnapping case regarding a baby taken from the Daniel Freeman hospital. I hoped you could give me some information."

"Oh yes, what about it?" Now I had her attention.

"Were you working there at that time?" I asked.

"Your voice keeps dropping out, but yes, I was there. I wondered if anyone would ever get around to calling me. I gave up after all these years."

"No one has contacted you about the kidnapping?"

"I was interviewed the following day for ten minutes, but that was the only time the police spoke to me."

"Do you have any thoughts or suspicions about who could have taken her?"

"Well, now that I've had years to think about it, I did think of a person that may have done it, but I have nothing to back it up."

"Can you give me a name?"

"I'm sorry, we keep breaking up, what did you say?"

73

I repeated the question.

"No, I'd rather not. I wouldn't want to falsely accuse someone."

"May I come visit you tomorrow, I promise to not pressure you. I only want to discuss the events of the kidnapping."

"Sure, Mister Canoe, I'll be here all day."

"Thank you, Missus Lerch, see you tomorrow, how's eleven or twelve sound?"

"Sure, that'll work."

I confirmed her home address, and then we both hung up. I leaned back, propped my feet on the coffee table and used the remote to turn on the TV. *Okay, I'll get the ID picture taken in the morning, go visit Mildred Lerch and then meet Ben at the restaurant parking lot in the evening. There's not much more I can do until I get more info on these people.*

The big news on TV was an accident and traffic jam on the 405. They showed the wreck and lanes of cars backed up as far as the camera could see. The odd thing was that cars were also at a standstill on the other side of the freeway where there was no accident.

The secondary news was about a drive by shooting outside a dance hall at Prairie and Imperial Highway. The police stated that although the street traffic was heavy and the parking lot and sidewalk was congested with party goers, no one saw anything. A clip was shown with a reporter asking grieving family members how they felt about their son's death. The film crew and reporter were shocked when the victim's mother threw a brick at them.

Twelve

Every three minutes they cut to a commercial with a yahoo in a cowboy hat hawking cars and singing, "Come see Cal." And in further news, a minor trembler shook the San Fernando Valley residents but only caused minor damage with no fatalities or reported injuries.

THIRTEEN

The following morning I did stretching exercises and push-ups. After showering, I looked in the phone book for photographers. I found one on Wilshire only three blocks from the hotel. They advertised fast service on passport photos, which would be ideal for the name tag. I decided to walk the short distance to the restaurant for breakfast and then to the photo shop. I rode the elevator down to the lobby and walked out the front door. I was almost to the restaurant when I heard honking behind me. I looked back out of curiosity and saw a gray sedan driving so slow that other drivers were honking and trying to get around him.

At first I thought that the driver was looking for somewhere to park, but he was passing empty spaces. The driver was now close enough that we were staring into each other's eyes. The driver suddenly got a panicked look on his face and floored it. His tires squealed as he careened around the corner past the restaurant. *That was strange,* I thought. Being naturally suspicious, I wondered, *is he tailing me?* I didn't recognize the driver, but noted that he was big and bulky looking with close cropped hair.

Thirteen

I went into the Country Kitchen and ordered eggs, bacon, hash browns and sourdough well toasted. I kept looking out the window but didn't see the gray sedan again.

After eating, I walked east toward the photo studio. It was a ten minute hike and I had to cross over to the other side of the street. The photographer shot and developed my picture in about twenty minutes while I waited. I kept an eye out as I walked back to the hotel, but there was no sign of the gray sedan. Probably nothing, I decided, but still, it was odd.

I felt all day yesterday that someone had eyes on me. The sensation that cross hairs were sighting in between my shoulder blades, gave me the uneasy feeling that someone was following me.

I have always possessed some innate sense of awareness that I'm sure saved my life many times in Vietnam. I firmly believe that it is some genetic DNA, inherited from my Osage ancestors, who survived eons of pursuing or being pursued.

I opened my map book and looked for the easiest route to Mildred's address in Gardena. *I've got plenty of time to go see Mildred, have a long talk, and still meet Ben later at Bob's Big Boy.* I went down to the garage for the car and headed for Gardena.

Cecil answered the phone, "It's Packy again, Mister Harding."

"Thank you Cecil," Harding said as he took the phone.

"Hello, Packy, what do you have for me?"

"I made a mistake, Mister Harding."

"Tell me what happened," Harding said, looking at Cecil and shaking his head.

"Well, this morning I was waiting in the hotel garage for him, when I see him walking by on the sidewalk. I got in my car and pulled out on the street and see him halfway down the block. I go along behind him but drivers behind me are honking because I'm driving too slow and holding up traffic. Well, I was getting nervous and didn't know what to do, and then I see Canoe had stopped walking. Then he turned around and looked directly at me. All I could do was take off fast down the street."

"Why didn't you follow him on foot?"

Packy paused, and asked, "You mean walk?"

"Yes, Packy, that's when you put one foot in front of the other."

"I'm sorry Mister Harding, I didn't think of it."

"Did he see you?"

"Yeah, he must have, he was looking right at me."

"All right, Packy, then what?"

"I didn't know what to do, so I went back to the hotel to wait for him."

"Quit dragging it out, what happened then?"

"When he didn't show up for an hour, I went out and drove around by the restaurant, looking for him. Since he was walking, I didn't think he could go too far. I couldn't see him, so after a while I went back to the hotel and…uh, now his car was gone. He must have come back and got it while I was out looking for him."

"All right," *Harding sighed,* "Wait and see if he returns, and please try to be a little more professional."

Thirteen

"Yes sir, Mister Harding."

Harding hung up without answering.

Jamie's mother wouldn't quit asking her about it. "What's it feel like? Do you do it all the time? Do you do it to me and I don't know about it?" Finally Jamie got fed up with the questions and told her mother, "I don't think I have that special ability any more. It's been getting weaker and weaker, now I think it's gone."

"Really?" Her mother asked.

"Yes, Mom, now I'm like everyone else. I'm glad it's over."

Her mother seemed disappointed, "Are you sure?"

"I'm absolutely sure, I've tried but I just can't do it."

"Try it on me, right now."

"Oh, Mom, come on."

They stared at each other for a minute. "See Mom, it doesn't work."

"Maybe it'll come back," her mother said, with some concern.

"Yes, could be, but I don't care."

Maybe she'll leave me alone now, Jamie thought.

FOURTEEN

I slowly drove down Mildred's street, looking for her address. When I spotted it, I pulled over to the curb. Her house sat toward the rear of a deep lot. I walked up the long driveway past a neighboring house on the left, where a woman and small boy were playing catch with a beach ball. The woman paused, and held the ball as she watched me approach the house.

"Do you know if Mildred is home?" I asked, taking the initiative.

She used her hand to brush her hair from her face and smiled.
"Oh yeah, Millie must be there, her car is in the driveway."
"Thanks, she's expecting me."
"Come on, Mom, throw the ball," I heard the boy yell.
They went back to the game with the mother apparently convinced that I wasn't an intruder.

The front porch was wood with railings. An ivy covered trellis was at each end. I stepped up on the porch and saw that the door was ajar about six inches. A small dog lay shivering in the opening with its head resting on its paws.

The dog lifted its head and whimpered. I reached down and patted its head.

"Hi, puppy, what's the matter?"

The dog stood, looked at me and whined again. Then it went back into the room, out of sight. I knocked on the door. When I got no response, I knocked again. Then I stuck my face up to the opening and yelled.

"Hello, is anyone there?"

I jerked my head back, *whoa, that doesn't smell good.* I recognized the sharp metallic odor of blood, a lot of it. I had smelled it too often in Vietnam. I shoved the door open, stepped in and pulled my tee shirt up over my nose and mouth. I could hear flies buzzing. The dog was standing in an open doorway looking back at me. The smell was stronger when I went into the kitchen where the flies were busy at their work.

The dog was lying at the feet of a woman that I presumed was Mildred Lerch. She was tied to a chair next to the kitchen table. Her ankles were tied to the front chair legs and her hands behind her back. The red oil cloth table cover was highlighted with bright yellow sunflowers. Its lively colors were in vivid contrast to the gory scene in front of me. On the table top I saw a butcher knife, an icepick and a pair of bloody pliers.

She had been tortured by a sadist. Whoever did this had enjoyed it too much. There's no way she endured all this without telling him what he wanted to know, if she had the answers.

Her head was tilted down with her chin resting on her chest. A bloody drool ran from her mouth down to her waist, staining the front of her blouse. Walking around her, I was careful to not step in the blood pooled on the floor. I walked from the kitchen down a hallway and checked out the two bedrooms and took a quick peek into the one bathroom. The house was empty.

I felt light headed, so I went to the sink, ran cold water and splashed it on my face. I used a paper towel to wipe with and went to the telephone. Using the towel, I picked up the phone and dialed the operator.

"I need the Gardena Police, it's an emergency."

A few seconds later, I heard, "Police, Sergeant Miller."

"Do you have a pen handy?"

"Well, yeah, whatta you want me to write?"

"I want to report a homicide."

The cop suddenly sounded more interested.

"What's the address?"

I gave him the address.

"Okay, I got it, what's your name?"

"I'll wait here," I said, and hung up the phone.

I went out and sat on the porch to wait for the cops to arrive. *This is something I never expected. While I'm investigating a thirteen year old kidnapping I get involved in a murder. I wonder if Mildred's torture and murder have something to do with the missing girl.*

The woman next door walked to the fence, the boy was bouncing the ball off the side of the garage.

"Is she there?" the woman asked.

"Yeah, she's here." I answered.

Five minutes later a patrol car skidded to a stop at the curb. The woman and I watched a young cop jump out and run to the porch.

"In there," I said, pointing at the door.

Fourteen

Seconds later the cop ran back out the door and puked over the side of the porch railing. The cop stood there for another twenty seconds, breathing deep, almost hyper-ventilating. He coughed and spat a couple times and then went to his car. I watched him open the passenger door, sit on the seat, and reach for his radio handset.

Five minutes later an unmarked police car pulled up. Two plainclothed detectives approached me. Another black and white parked behind them.

"Who are you?" One asked me, the other went inside.

"My name is Jacob Canoe. I'm the one that called it in."

"I'm Detective Ernesto Chavez, let me see your identification."

I handed him my ID identifying myself as a private detective. The cop studied it, and compared the picture with my face.

"What was your business here?"

"I had an appointment to interview her about a case I'm working on."

"Are you carrying a gun?"

"No," I replied.

The other detective came out of the house and approached Chavez.

"It's a homicide for sure. The victim's been dead for several hours and the blood is sticky to dry. She's been tortured."

"Frisk him," Chavez directed the other cop, nodding at me.

"How long have you been here?" Chavez asked me, while I was being patted down.

"He's clean," the cop said.

"I got here maybe fifteen minutes ago, that lady saw me arrive." I pointed at the woman, who was still standing at the fence.

Chavez looked at the other cop and nodded toward the woman. The cop walked over to interview her.

"Did you touch anything?" Chavez asked.

"The door was partially open when I arrived. I touched it with my hand to shove it further open so I could enter."

"Did you touch anything else?"

"Water faucet at the sink, then I used a paper towel to pick up the phone and dialed with the index finger of my right hand."

"Why'd you go in?"

"When I opened the door, I smelled the odor of blood and thought I better take a look."

"How did you know what the odor was?"

"I smelled it too many times in Vietnam. It's something I'll never forget."

Chavez nodded, "What's the case you're on?" He asked.

"It involves a missing baby, kidnapped from a hospital thirteen years ago."

Chavez paused from taking notes and looked at me.

"What was the victim's connection to the case?"

"She was a nurse at the hospital. She worked the OB ward at that time, but was off duty the night of the kidnapping."

The other cop returned. "She says he just got here, never saw him before."

Chavez handed my I.D. to the other cop. "Run him, see if he's clean."

By now a crowd of gawkers had gathered on the sidewalk. A uniformed cop was trying to break up the mob and send them on their way. Another two detectives arrived and entered the house.

Fourteen

"Why are you all the way from Kansas to work on this case?"

"An L.A. law firm hired us to look for the girl. Her grandfather wants to find her."

"What's the name of the law office?"

"Sorry, that's confidential." I answered.

The detective scowled at me.

"Do you think this murder could be connected to the missing baby?" he asked.

I shrugged. "I wouldn't think so. I hadn't told anyone I was coming here, including my boss but… anything is possible."

"Where are you staying?"

"The Savoir Regent on Wilshire, room 615."

Chavez paused, looking at me, "That's an expensive hotel."

"Yeah, well, they're paying for it."

The other cop returned. "He's legit, peep agency, out of Kansas."

"Okay Canoe, you're free to go."

I started for my car, when Chavez said, "By the way, Canoe, I remember that case from thirteen years ago, you'll never find her."

I shrugged, "You're probably right, Detective, but they're paying me to look."

Back in my car, I sat for a couple minutes wondering what to do next. My first lead had fizzled so I was getting nowhere fast. It was only one o'clock, so I decided to go back to my hotel. I had over three hours until my meeting with Ben.

Driving back, I was thinking of the cop's question about a connection to the kidnapping case, *I don't believe in coincidence, one crime may very well have something to do with the other. Is someone else looking for the girl? If so, how did they get here before me?*

85

FIFTEEN

At my hotel, I stripped, threw my clothes into the hamper, and took a long shower. After I toweled off, I called down to the front desk.

"This is Canoe in room 615. Give me a wake-up call at 3:30 this afternoon."

I stretched out on the couch and immediately fell asleep. I jolted awake when the phone rang and looked at the clock.

I picked up the phone, "Thanks," I said and hung up.

I got my car from the garage and headed for the rendezvous with Ben. The traffic was backed up at every intersection with at least two light changes. I kept checking my rear view mirror. Sure enough, a gray sedan always seemed to be a few cars behind me. I couldn't tell if it was the same one that I suspected of tailing me the day before.

I pulled into the restaurant lot and parked in a slot near the street. I looked around but didn't see the gray car anywhere now. *Maybe I'm imagining that I'm being followed. If so, there are a lot of gray cars in this town.* I checked my watch. *Ben should be getting off about now. He'll*

Fifteen

probably be here in ten minutes. I sat in my car until I saw the red truck pull in. Ben waved at me and parked a few spaces over. I got out of my car and stood next to the fender. After Ben got out of his truck, he walked toward me carrying a brown paper bag.

"Here's the uniform and name tag," he said. "You'll have to type in a name and insert your picture."

I opened the bag, looked in and saw a freshly laundered, folded uniform.

"I think that size will fit you," Ben said.

"Thanks Ben, I'll be coming in the front door at nine tomorrow, here's two hundred, I'll give you the rest in the morning."

"Another thing, Jake, after thinking about it, I remembered another name that wasn't on your list."

"Oh yeah, what do you have?" I asked, taking out my notepad.

"A woman OB doctor, her name is Janet Gresso."

"All right, spell it," I said. He did, and I added the name to my list, deleting the late Mildred Lerch.

I waited for him to leave, got into my car and checked the parking lot for the gray sedan. It was nowhere in sight so I started the car and pulled out onto the street.

After fighting the traffic for an hour, I finally made it back to my hotel. I stopped in the lobby.

"Hello, Jeff, do you have a typewriter I can use for a minute?"

"Sure, Mister Canoe, on the desk over there," he said, pointing toward the office.

I removed the paper insert from the I.D. tag, rolled it into the typewriter, paused and then typed on the name line-- "Cecil Harding."

I smiled at the irony. When I returned to my room, I inserted the photo into the badge. *Looks great*, I thought.

The phone rang, Cecil answered, "Mister Harding's office."

"Hi Cecil, it's me, Let me talk to the boss."

Harding took the phone. "Yes, Packy?"

"Mister Harding, I waited for Canoe and he got back to the hotel about 1:30. I decided to stay til about five or so to make sure he was in for the day. Well, a couple hours later, he comes back to the garage and leaves again."

"I hope you followed him."

"Yeah, I did, he drove back to the restaurant near the hospital. This is where it gets crazy, he don't go in, just waits in the parking lot. Then in comes that same red truck from yesterday and it parks next to him. Sure enough, it's the old guy he ate with yesterday. The old guy gets out and gives him a paper bag, they talk and then both leave. Then Canoe goes back to his room, and well, that's it."

"All right, Packy. Stick with him tomorrow."

I watched the usual carnage on the ten o'clock news that night. They led off with a fatal crash on the harbor freeway. Next up, one lane of the Hollywood freeway was shut down because of an oil spill at three p.m. Of course that incident resulted in traffic delays of up to two hours. A dozen illegal aliens were nabbed at a meat packing plant in East Los Angeles. In mid-town, an attempted bank robber was shot and killed

Fifteen

with the guard wounded. A twenty second spot reported that the body of an elderly woman was found in her Gardena home. Foul play is suspected, the victim has not yet been identified pending notification of family. Of course they keep running that damn commercial with the guy in a cowboy hat selling cars, "Come see Cal, come see Cal." I can't get the jingle out of my head.

I didn't sleep well with the vision of Mildred Lerch haunting me. I'm beginning to lean toward the possibility that her death has something to do with the missing baby. Someone else must be looking for the child, but how did they find Mildred and get to her before I did?

SIXTEEN

The next morning I drove to Bob's Big Boy in Inglewood for breakfast. After eating I went to my car and slipped the coveralls on over my street clothes. I pinned the I.D. badge on and drove to the hospital. As I turned into the parking lot, I saw a gray car behind me. The car continued past and down the street. I caught the profile of a large man with short hair. *I'm sure that's the same guy I saw two days ago,* I thought.

I parked and put on a baseball cap, then checked myself in the mirror. I was already wearing sunglasses. *Looks okay,* I thought.

When I entered the front door the guard glanced at me, smiled and nodded, as if he saw me every day. Ben was walking toward me. He raised his hand and waved. I waved back. The guard turned away to look out the door. *So far, so good,* I thought. I'm in with no problems.

I followed Ben past the elevators and down the hall to the storage closet. He pulled out the four wheel cart for himself and handed me a bucket and mop. No one took notice of us. We went to the service elevator and rode it down to the basement.

Sixteen

The basement was deserted and we walked past heating equipment, water boilers, ducts, pipes and other mechanical equipment. Ben unlocked a door at the end of the basement aisle.

"I'll be back in a half hour, will that be enough time?" Ben asked.

"It should be."

Once inside, I paused for a minute, letting my eyes adapt to the dim light. A row of windows along the top of the rear wall let in some light. I heard voices and could see legs from the knees down, going by. *There must be a sidewalk up there,* I thought. The cavernous room was full of filing cabinets except for one end which was stacked from floor to ceiling with boxes. There were desks and chairs piled up against another wall.

It appeared that the basement was used for not only archive files but storage of any unused or obsolete items. The walls were cement blocks and the floor was bare concrete. There was a slight damp musty odor. *Can't be too good for preservation of paper materials,* I thought. I turned on my pen light and started walking between the rows of filing cabinets, trying to decide where to start.

The air conditioning was minimal in the basement and I was feeling warm with the coveralls over my street clothes. I was starting to sweat so I ran my sleeve over my face to wipe away the perspiration. The cabinets were all dated and labeled as to contents. I hoped what I was looking for wasn't boxed up, if so, I'll never find anything. After skimming past purchases, outside services and utilities, I finally got to a row of cabinets labeled personnel. All the cabinet tops were covered with a fine layer of dust.

I moved down the aisle until I found a cabinet labeled for the year 1965. The cabinets were all standard with no locks which made my job easier. I rolled out the top drawer, and thumbed through files for doctors, surgeons, nurses and other medical technicians. I was in luck, they were categorized by departments. I worked my way down until I found obstetrics in the third drawer from the top.

Let's see, I thought, taking my notes out, *I've got three nurses and a woman doctor to look for.* I found all of them in a couple minutes, except for the doctor, Janet Gresso. I carried the folders to a table which was probably used for sorting. A lamp sitting on the desktop was going to give me plenty of light. I turned on the lamp and took out my Minox. It was a small camera, easy to conceal and took the sharpest pictures.

I opened the first folder for Gladys Crain and leafed through it. After setting aside payroll records, performance reports and time sheets I finally hit pay dirt. Her employee information sheet had an address, phone number, social security number and birth date. A bead of perspiration rolled down and dripped from the end of my nose. I wiped my face again with my sleeve. I laid the first sheet on the table, focused and snapped the picture.

I did the same with the other two files and returned them all to the cabinet. I started to put them back in the drawer from where I took them, then paused and thought about it for a few seconds. I walked down the row and buried them in the top drawer of a different cabinet. *No one else will be able to follow my trail.*

I returned to the original cabinet looking for anything on Doctor Janet Gresso. No luck, she wasn't anywhere. *That's it for now. I've got info on Emma Thomas, Roselda Flores and Gladys Crain. Mildred Lerch is dead. I'll call this information to Tom at the office and see if he can confirm the addresses or trace the social security numbers to new ones.* I used my shirt sleeve to wipe off any finger prints I may have left in the dust. I turned off the lamp and went to the door.

Sixteen

A few minutes later Ben rapped on the door.

"Jake, are you done?" He whispered.

"Yeah, good timing, let's get out of here. I'm dying from the heat."

We went to the elevator and I gave Ben the other two hundred. We rode up to the service hall and put the cleaning gear back in the storage closet.

I headed for the front door, putting my cap and sun glasses on. The guard nodded at me as I walked out. I took off the coveralls when I got to the car and looked around for Ben's red pickup. When I spotted it, I walked over, opened the driver's door and tossed the coveralls on the seat after removing the fake ID badge. I walked back to my car, got in and drove back toward the hotel.

I kept checking the rear view mirror and then I saw the car again, *uh, oh, there he is behind me. I'm going to have to deal with that guy soon.* Driving back I kept my eye on the rear view mirror. I would see the gray sedan and then it would drop back out of sight. A few minutes later, it would reappear.

When I got back to Wilshire Boulevard, I didn't see him behind me but I knew he was back there somewhere. I pulled down an alley next to the photo shop and parked in the rear lot. I went in and handed the clerk my Minox.

"I need the three shots on this roll developed and each printed on 8X10 sheets. I'll wait for them."

"I'm kinda backed up, can you come back later for them?" The clerk said.

"I really need them now, this should cover a rush job," I said, as I slid a fifty across the counter.

The clerk smiled, "Well, if they're that important, I'll get right on them, have a seat."

The clerk slipped the bill into his pocket. Thirty minutes later I had the prints and went back to my room.

Harding answered the phone. "It's me, Mister Harding," he heard Packy say.

"Hello, Packy, what do you have for me?"

"I followed Canoe to the restaurant by the hospital this morning. After he ate he went to his car and put on some work clothes of some kind and drove to the hospital. He went in and came back out about a half hour later. He went to his car, took off the work clothes and put them in a truck. I think it was the same truck the old guy was driving, it was the same color. I followed him back to the hotel. He must have turned off somewhere because I lost him about three blocks from the hotel. I went to the garage and he wasn't there so I waited and sure enough he showed up in a little while."

"Hmm, I wonder what he's up to. Just keep tailing him. We'll have to see where he takes us."

SEVENTEEN

I spread the file photos on the coffee table, *beautiful,* I said to myself. *I better call Tom right now, give him the social security numbers and have him put a trace on them.*

I picked up the phone and dialed the Wichita office.

The receptionist answered. "Hello Beth, let me speak to Tom." I said.

"One minute, Jacob, he'll be right with you."

I waited on hold until Tom came on.

"Hello Jake, how's the investigation going?" He asked.

I heard the usual annoying clicks and static on the phone.

"Not too bad, considering I didn't start with many facts. I've got names and social security numbers to be traced. I need any current addresses you can come up with."

"We've sure got a bad connection, Jake. Okay, I'm ready to write, go ahead and give me what you've got."

"Yeah, I know, Tom, this phone line is terrible with static."

I suddenly had a thought, "Hey, wait a minute, I'll call you back in a few minutes."

I left my room, and went down to the front desk.

"Jeff, I need quarters for the pay phone," I said, giving the desk clerk a five dollar bill.

I dialed the office, "It's me again. I need Tom."

When Tom came on, I said, "I'm back, on a pay phone in the lobby."

"What's going on? Why are we talking on a pay phone?"

"I suspect my room phone may be bugged." I explained how I found Mildred Lerch, tortured and murdered.

"I had called her the day before for an appointment to interview her, someone beat me to her. Now, I think I know how. If I hadn't called her, she would be alive."

"No Jake, don't do that to yourself, you didn't kill her. Someone else did."

"Tom, it had to be Harding and his crew. He's got a weasel named Cecil working for him and I think someone's tailing me."

"Can you find someone to check your apartment and phone for bugs?"

"Hey, Tom, this is L.A. I can get anything done here. I'm going to personally take care of the guy following me."

I read the names and Social Security numbers to Tom.

"When you get the info, leave a message with Jeff at the front desk. I'll call back for whatever you have."

"Alright, Jake, be careful, let me know what's happening."

I opened the phone directory hanging below the pay phone and searched through the many pages of detective agency listings. I found a small ad for an agency in Anaheim. I dropped in a quarter and dialed.

Seventeen

When his phone rang, Sid was leaning back in his chair, half asleep with both feet propped up on the desk. He almost fell over backwards trying to get the call. He fumbled at the phone and then composed himself.

"Ajax Investigations, Sid speaking."

"Hello, Sid, my name is Jacob Canoe, I'm a licensed P.I. from Wichita, Kansas. I'm working on a case here in L.A. and suspect my room has been bugged. I need someone to sweep it. Is that a service you can provide?"

"You called the right place Jacob, that's my specialty."

"How soon could you do it?"

"I'm kind of busy this time of the year, but I could squeeze you in tomorrow morning."

"That sounds good to me, Sid."

"All right, Jacob, give me a place and a time."

"I'm at the Savoir Regent on Wilshire, room 615. How about meeting me for breakfast at ten a.m.? There's a Country Kitchen restaurant a block east of the hotel, I'm buying."

"Yeah, I know where the place is, ten o'clock will be okay with me."

"What's your fee?"

"Well, let's see, it's an hour drive each way, and it'll take about…"

"You don't need to break it down, just give me a number."

"Uh, maybe three hundred, is that okay?"

"That's exactly the figure I had in mind."

"Thanks, Jacob, you got a deal, see you in the morning."

Sid hung up the phone, "*Great, I've got a client.*" He said to himself.

I stopped at the front desk as I headed back to my room.

"Jeff, can you have a large pepperoni pizza delivered to my room?"

"Sure thing, Mister Canoe, I'll call it in now."

I stayed in my room the rest of the day, nursing the pizza, washing it down with beer. I still couldn't get the image of Mildred Lerch's tortured body out of my head. The bug had to have been installed by Harding or someone he hired. *If I had been more cautious Mildred would be alive. I'll keep looking for the girl, but I will not let Harding or any of his goons get near her. There's something going on here that I'm not yet aware of. Whatever they want her for, I'm sure it's not her grandfather. What is so important that they would resort to torture?* The last vision in my mind as I fell asleep was of Mildred in that chair.

I don't know why I'm running. There is nothing but the jungle in front of me and when I look back, no one is behind me. I feel a flash of anxiety when I realize that I don't have my rifle. I think I hear someone gaining on me, but I glance back and nothing is there. I am close to the trees now and can see an opening in the foliage. A big cat is lying in the shade of the canopy watching as I run for the safety of the jungle. My heart is hammering and I can feel the blood pulsing in my ears. The cat lifts its head and looks at me with large yellow eyes. I run past the cat into the green jungle and collapse. I'm safe, nothing can get me now.

I'm standing again and see a path leading deeper into the dark jungle. I look back and the opening I entered is now closed, there is no retreat, I know the path ahead is intended for me. As I go deeper into the green abyss, I look behind me and the forest is folding closed behind me, leaving no way to go but the path ahead. No retreat is possible so I continue going forward until

Seventeen

I come to a fork in the path. To the left is a tangle of limbs and vines, to the right an open path.

Then I woke up in a sweat. I got up, went to the bathroom sink and splashed water on my face. After taking a few deep breaths, I returned to bed and fell asleep immediately.

EIGHTEEN

The next morning I went down to the lobby and out the front door. I started down the sidewalk, heading for the restaurant. As usual there was a lot of foot traffic. I was half way there when I got that familiar creepy feeling. I stopped abruptly and pretended to look in a window. Out of the corner of my eye I saw a man walking behind me. He stopped so fast he almost tripped.

I sauntered on to the restaurant, entered and was greeted with the aroma of frying bacon and waffles or pancakes. I returned a smile to the hostess.

"Take a seat anywhere," she said.

I slid into a booth near the window.

The man following me was strolling along looking in the windows. When he saw me looking directly at him, he got a startled look on his face and picked up the pace, disappearing around the corner. He was big, muscle going to fat, with short cropped hair. He was the same man I had seen driving the car yesterday.

The waitress set an empty cup in front of me, "Coffee?" she asked.

Eighteen

"Yes, I'm waiting for someone. We'll order breakfast later."

She poured my coffee and then moved to other tables topping off their cups.

A few minutes later I saw a short, stocky man come in and start looking around. *That's got to be him*, I thought, and waved him over.

I sized him up as he headed toward me. He was wearing glasses and sported a short military haircut not unlike mine. Even with a suit on, he looked powerful, like a weightlifter.

The man came over and asked, "Jacob?"

"Yep, I'm him. Please call me Jake, thanks for coming, Sid."

The waitress returned, poured Sid a coffee, and set menus on the table. We shook hands and exchanged business cards. After scanning the menus, we ordered our meals.

"So, what's going on with the bug in your room?" Sid asked.

"I was hired by an attorney to find a missing girl. They already had the room reserved for me when I arrived. I suspect that for some reason he had it wired."

"Why would they do that?" Sid asked.

"Beats me, to keep tabs on me, I guess."

"What's the attorney's name?"

"His name's Harding."

"Harding, huh, is it Baxter Harding?"

"Yeah, it is, do you know him?"

"Not personally, he's a two-bit shyster who started out doing grunt work for Mickey Cohen in the late forties. Word on the street was that he was a bagman for some of the local mobsters. He wasn't on the front line but stayed in the background trying not to get his hands too dirty. He also was involved with H.J. Caruso, a car dealer who was accused of shady dealings. Don't know where that went. Harding had somehow ingratiated himself with Mayor Sam Yorty, who may or may not have known of Harding's underworld connections. What little esteem Harding had, ended when Tom Bradley, who was elected Mayor in '73, kicked Harding out of his office."

"I didn't like him the first time I saw him, he radiated sleaze and his driver looked like an ex-con."

"Yeah, you want to watch your ass with him. I hope you got an advance."

"We did, a certified check, I wonder why he's really looking for the girl."

"There's got to be some money in it for him and it may not be good for her."

"Considering what he paid us to look for the girl, it must be a lot of money."

The conversation paused while the waitress set our meals on the table and refilled our cups. We waited for her to leave, than resumed our conversation.

"So what's the deal on the missing girl?" Sid asked.

I spent the next ten minutes explaining how we were hired to find the abducted baby.

"Yeah, I remember reading about that case some years ago. Every now and then the story gets a little ink in the papers. I can't imagine what he's after, if there's no real family involved, there can't be a large reward. Any reward from the police or F.B.I. is going to be minimal."

We finished eating and shoved our plates to the side. Sid reached for the ash tray, "Okay if I smoke?" He asked.

"It doesn't bother me, go ahead."

"I hope you don't mind me asking, how'd you get the scar?"

Eighteen

"Vietnam, just before I got out."

The waitress returned, removed the empty dishes from our table and refilled our cups.

"That's what I figured, how long were you there?"

"Nine years in the jungle, I took a two year extension and re-enlisted once."

"Damn, Jake, what the hell were you thinking?"

"Both of my parents were dead and I thought I'd found a home in the army. I finally wised up and got out of there."

"I was there too, but as soon as my time was up, I couldn't get out fast enough. I was lucky, I never got a scratch. All the guys said it was because I'm short, the bullets went over my head."

I slid three one hundred dollar bills across the table. "All right, Sid, let's head to my room and see what we can find."

I paid the cashier and we went to the parking lot.

"We'll walk to the hotel, if you don't mind leaving your car here."

"Okay Jake, I've got to get a piece of equipment out of my car."

Sid went to his car, unlocked the trunk, took out a briefcase and we headed for the hotel. I kept an eye over my shoulder as we walked but didn't spot the guy I suspected of tailing me.

When we got to my room, Sid said, "No conversation inside."

Sid took an instrument from his briefcase and flipped a switch. A red light began pulsing. The instrument had a ten inch probe extending from one end. I planted myself on a stool and watched Sid put the probe near the phone. The light went from blinking to a steady glow when it neared the phone. When he pulled the probe away, the light began blinking again. Sid pointed at the phone and nodded his head indicating it was bugged. Thirty minutes later Sid had gone completely through the place. He motioned me out to the hall.

"The phone is tapped. It picks up both sides of the phone conversation and voices in the room. Shall I remove it?"

"No, leave it. I want them to think I don't suspect anything."

"All right, thanks for the work, Jake. If you need anything else, give me a call."

"One other thing, Sid, see if you can locate a woman doctor by the name of Janet Gresso, will this cover it?" I asked, giving him another hundred.

"Sure, thank you," he said, slipping the bill in his pocket.

"I'll check back with you in a couple days." I said, as we shook hands.

I rode the elevator down with Sid and went to the pay phone. I dialed long distance and gave the operator the office number. After dropping in the required coins, I heard the ring and Beth answered.

"Hi, Beth, let me talk to Tom."

When Tom came on, I asked, "Did you have any luck on the names I gave you?"

"Yes, Jake, I've got current addresses for two, but not Flores. No phone numbers for any of them. You'll have to try to dig them out yourself."

"I've already searched the phone directory for these names, but no luck. I'll have to knock on doors."

I wrote the information he gave me in my Big Chief pad. *All right, now I'm getting somewhere,* I thought. *I can only hope I'll get some meaningful information from them.*

"Okay Tom, thanks, I had my room checked, the phone is definitely bugged. I left it as is, so they won't know for a day or two that I'm onto them. I'm going to get another place to stay and a different car, probably tomorrow or the next day. I'll let you know when I'm settled in."

"Okay Jake, be careful."

Eighteen

I returned to my room, opened the Thomas brothers map book and located the address for Gladys Crain, in Redondo Beach, and Emma Thomas in Hollywood. *Hollywood is the closest, I'll go there first.*

"Hello," Harding answered, when the phone rang.
"Mister Harding, this is Packy. I can't figure out what he's doing."
"I'll do the thinking, Packy, just tell me what happened."
"Well, he went to eat at the restaurant down the street like he always does. When he came back he was with this funny little guy." *I better not tell him that Canoe saw me, he'll really be mad.*
"What did they do, where did they go?" Harding asked.
"They walked back to the hotel and the little guy was carrying a brief case. Then they both went up to his room for about a half hour and then the little guy left."
"What was funny about him, what did he look like?"
"He had a suit on, with a bow tie. He looked like a salesman."
"Did you see his car and get his license plate number?"
"No, the guy was walking back to the café the last I saw him, carrying the brief case. I guess he was leaving."
"Okay, Packy, keep an eye on Canoe, let me know where he goes and what he does."

NINETEEN

It was already two p.m., I decided to wait a few hours, and then try to find Emma Thomas. I would get some dinner and take a tourist walk around Hollywood. I had no phone number for her so I would have to drop in unannounced. *I hope she'll be willing to talk to me.* About five o'clock I went down to the lobby expecting to see Jeff but a young woman was behind the front desk.

"Fresh coffee," she said, pointing to the urn on a side table.

"Thanks, I'll try a cup, where's Jeff?"

"He'll be back. We swapped shifts so I'm on until six p.m."

I poured a cup, loaded it with sugar and cream and sat on one of the leather couches.

I took a sip, "Good coffee," I said.

I watched her come around the desk. She was wearing a white long sleeved blouse and black slacks with matching vest. I figured the little black tie was an accessory provided by the hotel. Her hair was short cropped and jet black. She wore small diamond ear studs. She oozed sex.

She drew herself a cup, doctored it up, and sat next to me on the couch.

"Hi, I'm Alexis."

"Hello, Alexis, I'm Jacob."

"So Jacob, are you here on vacation or business?"

"Business."

"What do you do?"

"I'm a private detective, looking for a thirteen year old kidnapped girl."

She gushed excitedly. "Wow, a private detective, I've never met one before."

Naturally, I gave her a business card to show off.

"Hey, this sounds intriguing. Tell me about it, how long has the girl been missing?"

"Thirteen years, she was taken from the hospital when she was a month old."

"Is it a custody deal, did the father take the baby?"

She slid over a little closer, now I could smell her perfume.

"No, at least I don't think so, the father is unknown. The mother died in the hospital, so it appears to be a stranger abduction."

"Are you having any luck finding her?"

"I've got a few leads. I've got to check out a woman living in Hollywood who was a nurse at the hospital when the baby was taken."

"Where does she live in Hollywood? I know the town well."

I pulled out my scratch pad.

"Here's the address, but I don't know exactly where it is. I'll have to look it up in my map book."

She looked at the pad, "Vista Del Mar Avenue, I know exactly where it is. There are a lot of old apartment buildings along that street. I've got a map book behind the desk. I'll show you the easiest way to get to it."

We heard the desk phone ring.

"I gotta get that," she jumped up and ran around the counter to grab it.

I took the last swallow of my coffee and tossed the Dixie cup into a waste basket.

"I'm going up to my room," I said, "See you before I leave."

I looked back when I was getting into the elevator, she smiled at me.

When I got to my room, I kicked back and contemplated getting out of this hotel. A small place on the beach would be great, but first I'm going to discourage the guy tailing me. I'm tired of looking back over my shoulder and seeing that car. I may have to hurt him a little, not too much, only enough to convince him to be more afraid of me than Harding. He should not be difficult to confront, since he's a failure at surveillance.

At 5:30, I showered and got dressed. Chinos, light blue chambray shirt and casual dinner jacket, no tie. At 5:55, I took the elevator down to the lobby. Alexis was talking to a couple at the counter, so I sat on the couch to wait. The elevator door opened and Jeff came in, probably from the garage.

He smiled and waved, "Hello Mister Canoe."

The two guests left for the elevator just as Jeff went around the desk. Alexis waved me over.

"I had a thought," she said. "Parking can be a bummer in that neighborhood. You'd be smarter to take a cab. The driver could take

Nineteen

you right to the address. Or if you want, I could go along and help you find it."

I saw Jeff looking at me enviously as I chatted with Alexis. It was obvious that he had a fondness for her.

"Thanks for the offer, Alexis, but I may have a few other places to go."

She looked disappointed, but they both waved as I went out the front door to the curb. *Good luck Jeff,* I thought.

A minute later I was in a cab heading for Hollywood. I gave the driver the address.

"It's about twenty five minutes, depending on the traffic." He said.

Cecil answered when the phone rang.

"It's the girl from the hotel," he said, handing the phone to Harding.

"Hello, Alexis, did you get any information for me?"

"Not much, Mister Harding, he's going to Hollywood to look for someone on Vista Del Mar, but he didn't tell me the name. He was pretty close-lipped about it and I couldn't get him to take me with him."

"You didn't overplay it, did you? Did he suspect you?"

"No way, they never suspect sweet little me."

"That's okay, Alexis, don't worry, I know who he's looking for, she's no longer living there."

"Sorry I don't have any more information for you, Mister Harding."

"That's fine, Alexis, goodbye."

When we pulled up to the address, the cabbie asked. "Shall I wait?"

"No," I answered, "I might be a while. I'm going to walk over to the strip later."

After paying the fare, I watched him drive off. The two rows of slump block cottages, that had seen better times, were divided by a cracked cement walk extending to the alley. Only a few of the units had screen doors and the remaining ones were torn and ratty looking. This was probably a motor court back in the 40's but was now being used for month to month rentals.

Each individual address was above the door. The one I was looking for was at the very end, next to the alley. When I knocked on the door, two feral cats yelped and scrambled out of a trash dumpster. The dumpster was backed up to a cement block wall next to the apartment. I watched the cats disappear under a large oleander bush. I waved my hand in front of my face to dispel the odor from the bin.

The door opened about four inches, "Whatta you want?" a voice snarled.

Her hair was grey and scraggly, her voice hoarse, ravaged by years of too much booze and too many cigarettes. She glared at me with an angry look.

"I'm trying to find Emma Thomas, is that you?"

A little terrier looking mutt stuck it's snout out the door opening and growled at me.

"Shut up," the woman shouted, and then grunted when she gave the dog a vicious kick. I heard the dog's diminishing howls as it headed for safer quarters.

"Never heard of her." The woman said, as she started to close the door.

I re-checked the number over her door.

"Your address is the one I have for her."

"I only been here six weeks, she must've been here before I moved in."

She started shoving the door closed again.

"Do you have a manager on site?" I asked.

"Up front," she said, pointing toward the entrance.

"Okay, thank you ma'am." I said.

She slammed the door, and I heard her screaming at the poor little dog as I walked away. I found the manager's apartment. It was the first apartment I had walked by when I arrived.

A man's voice answered when I rapped.

"Just a minute, I'll be right there."

There was some shuffling around, and then the door opened.

A grizzled old man in need of a shave opened the door. He was squinting through a pair of glasses with one bow missing. The eyeglasses were perched on his nose at an awkward angle. The remaining bow was hooked over his right ear. It was more pitiful than comical. He was gripping the handles of one of those four wheel walkers. His sleeveless undershirt was streaked on the front with what looked like coffee stains. His baggy trousers were held up by a belt tightly cinched around his waist. The belt was too long with the tail hanging about six inches below the buckle. He was wearing socks with his big toes poking through holes.

He looked me over as if I was an alien from another world or time. He didn't speak, he only stood there slack jawed, staring at me. His breath reeked from a combination of cigarettes and alcohol.

I finally spoke. "Hello, my name is Jacob Canoe. I'm trying to find Emma Thomas. I have her address as the apartment on the end."

"She's dead," he said, "Going on two months now."

No surprise, I thought, *this is the end of the line for the human detritus that society has no more use for. Most of these tenants are living on a meager social security check. The few that are working are afraid that their next pay envelope will contain the dreaded pink slip. They will find that they have been replaced by someone that will do their job for fifteen cents an hour less. All their youthful hopes, ambitions, and dreams have withered down to a miserable day to day existence. Now they are passing each tortuous night in solitude, waiting for that final tap on the shoulder.*

"What happened to her?" I asked.

"Some psycho got in there and did her in, made a real mess of the place. I had to get a crew in to clean it up. The slumlord that owns this dump threw a fit when he got the bill."

"So she was murdered?"

"Yeah, took a week to air the place out after it was cleaned. Whoever did it must have really been pissed, it was savage."

"Well, thank you for your help."

"I was hoping you were related to her and was going to take her suitcase out of the storeroom, I need the space."

"Didn't I mention that I'm her nephew? I'll take it off your hands."

I don't know if he believed me or not but he didn't seem to care, he wanted to get rid of the suitcase.

"I'll get the key."

I watched him roll the walker to the wall behind him and remove a key from a board full of keys with tags. He trundled back and handed the key to me.

"The storeroom is off the alley near the dumpster. It's a cheap brown cardboard suitcase. A tag with her name is tied to the handle. Don't forget to bring the key back, just drop it in my mail slot."

He shut the door as I walked away. I heard a dead bolt slam into place.

I unlocked the storage room door, went in and felt around for the light switch. When I found it and flipped it on, it lit a dim, probably forty watt light bulb. The room was full of boxes, suitcases, two old refrigerators and a lot of other junk. I dug around and came up with the one described by the manager. The tag said Emma Thomas.

I set the suitcase in the alley, closed and locked the storage door. I undid the buckles and opened it next to the dumpster. I pulled wads of clothes out and piled them on the gritty, sand covered asphalt alley floor. I leafed through a sheaf of papers, none of any significance. I was ready to give up when I noticed a pocket on one end. I reached in, felt something and pulled it out. It was a small address book. I flipped through it, saw addresses and phone numbers so I slipped it into my jacket pocket.

I heard footsteps behind me. I looked around and saw two winos heading my way. When they were close, I could see what looked like vomit on one guy's shoes.

"Hey man, this is our alley."

"Get lost," I said.

"Anything in that dumpster is ours, Dude."

"I'm leaving, you guys got two choices, you can drop the threatening attitude and I'll give you this suitcase and clothes, or I'm going to make you wish you never met me."

"All right man, be cool, we'll take the goods."

When I walked away, I heard one of them say, "Hey, this is all women's shit."

"Don't matter, we can sell it." The other guy answered. I dropped the key in the manager's mail slot like he asked. When I reached the front side walk, I laughed when I heard one of them yell, "Hey Dude, don't come back or we'll really get you next time."

I walked south a block and turned right on Hollywood Boulevard. I walked west a couple blocks, then south to Sunset Boulevard. I was looking for a place to grab something to eat. Most of the cafés served liquor and noisy drunks were cheering baseball games. I finally chose a small restaurant that was quiet and fairly smokeless. I opted for fish and chips and was quite surprised at the generous plate of deep fried cod. After eating, I walked east to Vine, enjoying the freak show.

The street was crowded with both male and female prostitutes, haunting doorways and lined up along the curb. A trio of tough looking butch lezbos, tricked out in leathers and chains, glared at me as they passed. I stepped aside for a ludicrous, balding, middle aged man skipping down the sidewalk. Then I came face to face with a tall dark haired woman in heels. She had in tow a small blond girl in pigtails. At first glance, the girl appeared to be a teenager, but upon closer inspection, I could see she was was older. She had a leather collar around her neck with a chain attached. The tall woman had hold of the other end of the chain. She smiled when she saw me staring at the girl.

"Hi stud, cute, isn't she?"

"Well, yeah, what's the deal?" I asked.

"The deal is, she's yours, if you want her. She'll do anything I tell her to do."

"Uh… no thanks, I'll pass." I said.

Nineteen

That was it for me, I hailed a cab and thirty minutes later was back in my room. Tomorrow I would head for Redondo Beach to see Gladys Crain.

Jamie was spending more time out on her own. Especially now that her mother thought that she had lost her special ability. She was no longer afraid that anyone would discover what she could do. She hid it well and this gave her a feeling of power. She had taken to riding city buses on different routes listening for voices. Every now and then she would hear something that reinforced her belief that others like her were out there. The thought somewhat worried her and she wasn't sure she wanted to have any contact with anyone like her.

The last few nights she had been having strange dreams. The dreams were a little unsettling, although she didn't feel frightened, only puzzled. There was only an old man looking at her, his face was kind, almost compassionate. He had long white hair and the appearance of an American Indian. He never said anything, just looked at her.

On the other hand, her waking hours had become more worrisome since the dreams started. She had been feeling uneasy, as if awaiting some impending doom to befall her. She had not told her mother, who already fretted enough for both of them. But Jamie was trying to be more cautious and aware of her surroundings. She felt something bad was about to happen.

TWENTY

Before I left for Redondo Beach, I flipped through the address book from Emma Thomas's suitcase. The book appeared to be very old with a cracked leather cover. It was filled with names, addresses, phone numbers and pages of recipes and undecipherable notes. Nothing jumped out at me so I put it back in my pocket for later scrutiny.

I took La Brea south to Imperial Highway and then west to Highland Avenue. I wanted to take the scenic route along the beach. I had just turned left on Highland and was heading south when I checked the rear view mirror. Sure enough, I spotted the gray sedan two cars behind me. *I'm getting fed up with this guy following me.* I thought. *I'm going to deal with him now.*

When I passed Rosecrans, the street was lined with multi-storied apartments and condos on the right between Highland and the ocean. Between each building was a small street or alley leading down to the beach or to an alley. I pulled over to the curb and watched the gray car drive pass and park about six cars down. I got out of my rental and

Twenty

walked toward the other car, but before I reached it, I turned right and went down a small street.

The street was steep and had steps on each side for foot traffic. As soon as I was around the corner and out of sight, I raced to the alley at the end of the building, turned right, and then ran to the other end and back up to Highland. When I got back to the street that I first went down, I looked around the corner and saw the big guy that had been following me.

The man was almost to the bottom of the steps, with his back to me. The traffic on Highland was probably what prevented him from hearing me as I came down behind him. He had stopped at the alley and was peering around the corner.

I was about three steps above him, his back stiffened when he heard me speak. "I'm here," I said, as I kicked him in the middle of the back.

He stumbled across the alley to the far wall. He put his hands up to keep from falling or smashing into the wall. I was on him before he could react and drove his face into the wall. I heard him grunt when his nose broke. Then I reached around him, did a quick pat down, pulled a gun from the man's shoulder holster and punched him in the kidneys.

He wheezed and his knees buckled. I spun him around and gave him two quick jabs to the ribs, then stepped back and watched him slide down the wall to a sitting position. I squatted down next to him.

"Please don't hit me again," he pleaded between deep breaths.

"Why are you following me? Are you working for Harding?"

"Yeah," he gasped, "I was only supposed to follow you and tell him what you did."

"What's your name?"

"Paul Kotski, they call me Packy. I wasn't going to hurt you or anything, just see where you went."

"Packy, tell me why he wants to find the girl?"

"I don't know, he doesn't tell me anything. I heard them say, she's worth a lot of money."

"What do you know about Mildred Lerch, did you murder her?"

"I never heard of her and I didn't kill anybody. I wouldn't do that."

"Let me see your wallet, Packy."

He winced as he lifted himself up and pulled it from his hip pocket. He handed it to me and lowered himself back to a sitting position.

I removed his driver license. "Is this your current address?"

"Yeah, it is."

I wrote the address in my note pad.

"Packy, how do you want to define our relationship?"

"Uh… what do you mean?"

"Come on Packy, is our relationship going to be based on friendship or confrontation?"

"Uh… friendship, I want to be your friend."

"That sounds good to me, Packy. You're not going to follow me again, are you?"

"No, I promise, I won't."

"You know what's going to happen if you do, don't you?"

"Uh… you're going to hurt me?"

"That's right, Packy, only worse next time."

I stuck the license back into his wallet and dropped it on his lap. A door opened down the alley. A man stuck his head out and looked at us.

Twenty

"What's going on?" He yelled.

"This man's been hurt, call an ambulance," I answered.

I went back up to Highland and jotted down the license plate number of the gray car. Then I opened the driver's door and shoved the gun under the front seat. I left in my car and headed south toward Gladys Crain's house in Redondo Beach. I pulled over to the curb when an ambulance going the other way passed me, it was heading north, with siren blaring.

I found Gladys's house in Redondo Beach. I had no phone number so I couldn't call in advance, but hoped she would talk to me. I walked to the door and rang the bell.

A large woman opened the door. She glared at me with her hands on her hips. *Great*, I thought, *I'm making enemies everywhere I go.*

"Hello, my name is Jacob Canoe. Are you Missus Crain?"

"No, I'm her nurse, she don't see nobody," she started to close the door.

I heard a voice from inside the house, "Who is it?"

"Tell her I want to talk about the missing baby, from the hospital."

"Some man, it's about a missing baby," the nurse answered.

After a few seconds hesitation, I heard the woman again.

"Okay, let him in, I'll talk to him," the voice said.

The nurse scowled at me, "All right, come on in."

She led me through a small living room, down a dark hall and into an even darker bedroom with the window shade pulled down.

"Don't trip over that tube on the floor," the nurse advised me.

I saw a plastic tube running from an oxygen bottle to the bed. Gladys Crain was propped up in a hospital type bed. One of those you can crank up, so the patient is sitting upright. Gladys turned on a bed side lamp. I could see that she had an apparatus hanging around her neck with tubes stuck up her nostrils. The lamp table next to her bed also held an ashtray the size of a Buick hubcap. It was almost overflowing with butts. A pack of Lucky Strikes and a Zippo were next to the ash tray.

The room smelled of stale smoke and urine. My eyes were adjusting to the dim lighting. A six drawer dresser was standing against one wall. The top was covered with an array of pill bottles. A closet door was wide open with a pile of laundry lying on the floor in front of it. A one foot tall stack of magazines and newspapers was on the floor next to the bed. I did a double take when I saw the top magazine was a copy of Architectural Digest.

"Missus Crain, my name is Jacob Canoe and I'm investigating a baby's disappearance from Daniel Freeman Hospital. I understand you worked there at that time."

"Are you with the police?"

"No, I'm a private investigator. The child's grandfather is trying to find her." I decided to stick with that story. I no longer believe it but it's all I have to go with.

I gave her a business card and showed her my ID.

"Well, I'm glad you're not a cop, you might get something done. Yes Jacob, I worked there, but not that night. She was a beautiful little girl with auburn hair and light green eyes. It was awful when she went missing."

"I know you weren't there at the time of the abduction, but what do you remember hearing about that night?"

Twenty

"All I know is that Emma Thomas and Rosie Flores were on duty. We had a certain schedule to follow for bed checks and so forth. As far as I know they followed all the rules. Whoever took the child had to have known the routine and took advantage of a small window of opportunity."

"Do you have any suspicion of who might have taken her?"

"No. I have no idea."

"Would you take a look at this list of nurses and tell me if you know of any other names I can add to it."

Gladys studied the list for a while and handed it back to me. "I see you have a line drawn through Emma Thomas, did you talk to her?"

"She is deceased, I'm sorry. I guess you didn't know about it."

"No, I hadn't heard. What a shame."

"What about the other names?"

"I don't see Millie's name."

"If you mean Mildred Lerch, I'm sorry, she's also dead," I answered.

"Oh my, what happened to her?"

I paused, and then answered. "She was murdered."

"Well, heavens, two of my friends gone." Gladys said, shaking her head.

"What can you tell me about the reaction when the girl went missing? I understand some of the nurses were almost hysterical."

She looked at the nurse, "Clara, could you leave us alone for a few minutes?"

The nurse frowned and stalked out of the room in a huff.

"Go close the door, Jake, that busybody thinks she has to know everything."

I pushed the door shut, returned and sat next to the bed.

Gladys reached for her cigarettes. I waited while she lit up. She inhaled and started coughing. Her face went red and she began wheezing. I considered calling the nurse but her breathing steadied and she began to relax.

"These damn smokes are going to kill me some day."

That's for sure, I thought. *That day is coming faster than she can imagine.*

"Well, the thing is, I thought I could read her mind." Gladys had lowered her voice to a whisper.

"Read the baby's mind? Explain that to me," I said.

"I always seemed to know when she wanted anything. I knew when her diaper needed to be changed, when she was hungry or just wanted to be picked up and held. But I also knew at the time, the idea that I was able to read her mind seemed crazy."

"What about the other nurses, did they feel the same way?"

"I think they did but we never talked about it. Then I finally figured out what was going on. I wasn't really reading her mind."

"What was going on?"

"She was projecting her thoughts into my mind."

She doesn't think that sounds crazy? I thought.

"How does that work?" I asked. "A baby can't formulate words."

"It's like when you're hungry, you don't have to actually think the words 'I'm hungry,' you just know you are."

"So, you believe the child was somehow communicating her emotions or feelings to you."

"Yes, that's it, that's a better way to put it, and I'm sure the others felt it too, that's why everyone was so distressed when she went missing."

Twenty

This case is getting weirder by the day, I thought, *now a baby with ESP.*
"Do you have Rosie's phone number? All I have is her address."
"Sure, I'll look it up for you."
After thumbing through her personal address book, Gladys read the number to me. I wrote it in my note pad.
"Do you want me to call her for you?" She offered.
"Yes, thank you, Gladys. May I have a glass of water?"
Breathing the smoke was starting to irritate my throat.
"Clara, get Jacob a glass of water," she yelled.

I walked to the kitchen and waited while Clara poured the water. I sat at the table and sipped the water. *Not much information from Gladys but I did get a phone number for Roselda Flores, and I could hear Gladys talking to her on the phone.*
"Hey, Jacob, what time are you going to be there?" She yelled at me.
"About ten tomorrow morning, if that's okay."
I finished the water and returned to the bedroom.
"She said ten is okay, she'll be looking for you."
"Is it okay if I come back to see you again? I may have more questions."
"Jacob, I just remembered another name that's not on your list. A young temp named Ann. I can't think of her last name, she only worked with us a few weeks. I'm not sure she was even there at the time the baby was taken. I think her last name started with a G, like Gilmore or something like that. Some of the girls called her Annie. If I remember right, she and Rosie were pretty close so Rosie might know her full name and how to find her."

"This is the first time I've heard of her."
"Like I said, she was a temp, hired through an agency."

"Okay, thanks Gladys." I added to the information in my note pad.

"So long, Jacob, and yes, you're welcome to come back if you have more questions."

I left and headed back north on Highland Avenue. When I passed the gray car, I saw it was still parked where Packy had left it. I continued on to the small town of El Segundo and spotted a beach front motel with a vacancy sign. It advertised rooms by the day, week or month.

I pulled into the parking lot. It was an older looking place with white washed cabanas and red tiled roofs. There were only a few cars parked in front. Since it was right on the beach, I figured it probably filled up at the weekend. When I stepped out of my car I could hear the surf and smell the salty sea air.

Cecil answered the phone and heard Packy blurt out, "I gotta talk to Mister Harding."

"It's Packy, he don't sound too good." Cecil said, handing the phone to Harding.

"Hello, Packy, what's going on now?"

"I quit, Mister Harding, he caught me following him."

"What do you mean, you quit?"

"I don't want anything to do with that guy."

"Did you tell him that you work for me?"

"I didn't have to, he already knew."

"What else did he say?"

"Not much, he asked about the girl and I told him I don't know anything about her, and one other thing, Mister Harding."

"Yes Packy?"

Twenty

"You better be careful, he hurt me worse than I've ever been hurt and he didn't break a sweat."

"Where are you now?"

"I'm at Torrance Memorial Hospital, an ambulance brought me here and I'm not going to follow him anymore."

"What's wrong with you?"

"Broken nose, cracked ribs, he beat me up bad."

"Where's the car?"

"It's parked on Highland, just south of Rosecrans, on the west side."

"Okay, I'll have it picked up. Shall I send Cecil for you?"

"No, they won't let me leave until I quit pissing blood. Like I said, I quit, I'll find my own way home." He hung up.

"Hmm, Cecil, I think we underestimated Canoe. Call Chicago right away, get those guys we used before. I want them on the next plane out."

TWENTY ONE

Jamie often wondered, *am I really the only one? There must be others.* Several times, in a crowd, she would hear something, a tiny voice in her head or someone humming a tune. She would look around, silently asking with her own mind. "Are you there? Who are you? Can you hear me?" There was never an answer and as the contact faded away she would experience a feeling of disappointment. *I used to think that maybe someday I'll find another like me, but now I'm ready to give up on that idea.*

And then one day while riding a bus, she heard low voices, quiet whispers, murmurs. The voices asking, "Where are you, we know you're near. Show yourself to us." The persistence was menacing and almost frightening, not what she expected. Suddenly she no longer had the desire to contact anyone for fear they wanted to harm her. Staying in crowds and not reacting to the voices now seemed safer. She wanted to hear them, but not have them hear her or know who she is. She didn't respond to the voices and continued looking out the window, afraid any reaction would give her away.

Twenty One

When the bus stopped a group of riders rose to get off, so Jamie stood, went down the aisle and stepped off with them. An elderly woman, using a walking cane headed in one direction with Jamie keeping pace alongside her. *Maybe they'll think I'm with her,* she thought. The others passengers scattered, some going the opposite way and some crossing the street. Jamie couldn't resist looking back and saw two men and a woman, get off the bus after the others and look both ways. She quickly looked straight ahead and kept walking. She was almost at the corner when she heard the bus drive away. She snuck a quick peek back and saw one of the men point at her. As soon as she turned the corner she took off running. After two blocks her breath was getting ragged and she was getting a stitch in her side. She looked back and saw that one man was gaining ground on her and the others were close behind. An alley was coming up so she turned abruptly to her left and ran into the alley hoping for a place to hide. She immediately realized she had made a mistake, the alley was a dead end with brick walls on both sides. There was no exit out except the way she came in. She spotted a dumpster and squatted behind it. The footsteps had slowed and were nearing her.

"She's here," someone said.

What am I doing, she asked herself, *how long can I hide behind this dumpster? Those people will find me in a minute, so s*he reluctantly stood, exposing herself.

They were about fifteen feet away, staring at her. Jamie was suddenly angry, *why should I have to run, what right do they have to chase me?*

"Get out of my way, leave me alone," she screamed at them.

To her amazement, the three moved to the sides of the alley with their backs against the building walls. The woman was on one side, the men on the other.

Now she realized the truth, *they're afraid of me. They can't hurt me.*

"Don't look at me," Jamie said angrily.

They all tilted their heads down and stared at their shoes while Jamie walked past them and out the alley.

TWENTY TWO

El Segundo is named for the site where Standard Oil Company built their second California refinery. It's a refuge treasured by residents looking for the small town life. On the negative side El Segundo has a sewage treatment plant on the beach, which creates an unpleasant odor when the wind is blowing inland.

I went into the motel office and saw a tough looking older man behind the counter. On the wall were plaques, one said "Air Borne." There were pictures of soldiers in uniform.

"You must be a veteran." I said, eyeing the faded tattoo on his arm. It was a parachute with an eagle on top and a banner underneath saying 101st.

"Yep, European theater, I dropped in for the D-day invasion. You look battle tested yourself." He said, glancing at my scar.

"Yeah, I was in Vietnam, my name's Jake Canoe."

He stuck his hand out, "Always glad to meet a fellow soldier. My name's Andy, need a room?"

"Yes, I'll be staying several days, maybe a week."

Andy led me to a room on the beach side away from the Highland Avenue traffic. It was a standard one bedroom, one bathroom cottage with a queen size bed, side table and lamp. There was no couch or kitchen like the hotel. There was a small writing table with a lamp and chair. The walls appeared to be freshly painted and the carpet looked new.

"It ain't too fancy but it's clean and it is quiet back here." Andy said.

"It'll do just fine, Andy. Can you get me a phone?"

"Sure, Jake, and I always have the coffeepot on, so come to the office anytime and we'll swap war stories."

"Thanks Andy, if I'm not here, come on in, and set the phone on the table." I paid for a week and the phone deposit, he handed me the key.

"Will do, Jake, the phone will be here when you get back." he said, closing the door behind him.

I returned to my car and drove north to the airport where I pulled into a Hertz car rental agency. Five minutes later I had completed the paperwork and a woman working the counter gave me the key. I told her that I would be back for the car later. I drove Harding's car back to the hotel to get my clothes.

When I got to the Savoir Regent, I parked Harding's car in the garage. I dropped the keys on the driver side floor, left the car door unlocked and rode the elevator up to my room.

I packed my suitcase, picked up the map book and Big Chief tablet from the table and tossed them in on top of my clothes. I looked around to make sure I had everything, locked the door and went down to the lobby. I had Jeff retrieve my money envelope from the safety deposit box and call a cab for me.

Twenty Two

I gave Jeff a twenty and said, "You haven't seen me and don't know when I left or where I went."

"I've got it, Mister Canoe."

When the taxi arrived, I climbed in and told the driver. "Take me to the airport."

At the airport, I paid the cabbie and walked across the street for my rental car. I showed my papers to the counter attendant, went to the car, threw my suitcase in the trunk and left. I drove back to my motel room in El Segundo and parked next to the cabana. I went in, unpacked and hung up my clothes. The phone was already in my room. It was midafternoon in Wichita so I called the office. Beth answered, and then Morgan came on.

"Hello, Jake, how's the investigation going?"

"I've got a couple leads to track down tomorrow. Emma Thomas was murdered two months ago at her home in Hollywood, so that went nowhere."

"Murdered, huh, do you think that has anything to do with the case?"

"Hard to tell, but it's starting to look like a pattern."

"Are you still being tailed?"

"Not any more, I had a talk with the guy and we came to an agreement. He's not going to follow me anymore, and I promised not to use him as a punching bag."

"Was he working for Harding?"

"Of course he was."

"What do you think Harding's up to?"

"I haven't figured it out yet and the guy tailing me didn't know what was going on with the girl."

"Did you believe him?"

"Oh yeah, no way he was going to lie to me."

"Harding's angle on this is puzzling, what does he have to gain?"

"I'm sure there's really no grandfather, there's something else going on. I have information that Harding's had a shady past, and has been involved with a lot of illegal activity."

I decided not to mention the ESP angle. I hadn't figured that out myself.

"There must be money involved somewhere or he wouldn't have paid us so much to find her." Tom said.

"Yeah Tom, I agree, the guy following me didn't have a clue, he was only keeping tabs on where I went and who I saw."

"Did you get moved?"

"Yeah, and I've got a different car. Write this new address down."

I gave Tom the address and phone number.

"This phone number is for the motel office, he'll connect you with my room. If I'm not here, leave a message with the manager, his name's Andy, I'll call you back."

"One other thing, Jake."

"Sure Tom, what is it?"

I thought I knew what he was going to ask.

"How are you sleeping?"

"I'm sleeping fine, Tom, I think California agrees with me."

"Not having any nightmares?"

"I'm having nothing but sweet dreams, Tom."

He probably knows I'm lying.

Twenty Two

After a short pause, Tom answered. "All right, Jake, be careful and watch your back, I don't want you getting hurt."

"That I will, Tom, I'll check back tomorrow or the next day."

I took a shower, cranked up the AC a notch and stretched out for a nap. The thick cement block room walls and humming AC did a great job of muting out the street noise.

I smiled to myself as I drifted off. *Morgan sometimes seems to think I'm still that twelve year old kid he bailed out in 1950. I was shit scared back then and Morgan was the tough cop who covered for me and kept me out of big trouble. If it wasn't for Tom Morgan, I would probably have gone to reform school or worse. Neither of us imagined back then that I would someday be working for him. I often wonder how he joined the Wichita Police after the war in 1946 and by 1950 was the chief homicide detective. I asked about it once, he only smiled and winked. I figure he must know where some bodies are buried.*

TWENTY THREE

Cecil pulled up to the curb at LAX to pick up the Chicago guys. When he got out, the cop walked over, hitched up his pants and frowned.

"You can't park there."

"I'm going to pick some people up. I'll only be a couple minutes."

"No unattended cars at the curb, you'll have to park in the garage." The cop said, pointing to the parking structure.

Damn, Cecil thought, *I hate parking in there, it takes twice as long.*

"All right, Officer, I'm leaving."

Cecil pulled from the curb and moved into the left turn lane for the garage. Another driver honked at him, annoyed that Cecil cut him off. The lane slowly moved ahead one car at a time until he reached the parking ticket dispenser. He pulled a ticket out and drove in when the arm swung up. He followed all the other cars looking for a slot and ended up on the top floor where he finally found a parking space. The whole process took thirty minutes. *I'm probably late,* he thought. *This place is worse than the Del Amo Mall the day before Christmas.*

Twenty Three

When he got to the elevators there was a mob waiting to go down to the street level. Another five minutes went by until he was finally able to shoulder his way in. Everyone was in a foul mood so he garnered a few dirty looks which he ignored. The elevator stopped at every floor on the way down, where another one or two people tried to squeeze in. A phalanx of angry riders blocked the entrance and wouldn't let anyone else on at the last two floors. Cecil finally made it out of the garage and to the crosswalk.

When he entered the airport lobby he saw the three men glaring at him.

"Where the hell you been?" one of them asked.

"Sorry, they wouldn't let me park at the curb, I had to park in the garage."

"You shoulda left earlier."

"I know, but it took a while to get parked."

"I suppose we gotta carry our suitcases," another asked.

"I'm sorry, if you want to wait at the curb, I'll go get the car."

"Naw, forget it, let's get going."

TWENTY FOUR

George Enders picked up his phone, "Agent Enders." He answered.
"Hello, George, this is Howard Kent over here at Parker Center."
"Hey, Howard, what's up?"
"Are you CIA spooks still delving in that ESP stuff?"
"We don't call it that anymore, Howard. It's now called paranormal studies."
"Oh yeah, and you don't think that also sounds a little weird for a government agency program?"
"Yeah, maybe, did you call me to discuss semantics?"
"No, how about we meet for lunch? I may have something for you."
"Pertaining to…what?"
"An old case, that possibly involves ESP."

"All right Howard, now you have my attention. I can be out of here in about fifteen minutes. Is that okay?"
"Sure, that'll work, I'm at my office. It's walking distance to the cafeteria across from Union station?"

Twenty Four

"I'm on the way, see you there."

Enders arrived before Kent and waited at the entrance. He watched Kent approach, and stuck out his hand for a shake. They went in the cafeteria. Each grabbed a tray and got in line. Without a word, they filled their trays and went to a table near the window.

"So, Howard, is this really about ESP, or your way of getting a free lunch?"

"Both," Kent answered, with a smile.

"You couldn't tell me on the phone?"

"I don't like talking to you on your phone, I suspect it's bugged."

"Yeah, I know what you mean."

"I guess you know that we have certain subjects that are flagged. We're supposed to call your office when we have activity regarding said subjects."

"Do you have something flagged for me in particular?"

"Not you personally, it's for your office, I wanted to give you first shot."

"Okay, Howard, what have you got?"

"This is regarding a baby, kidnapped from a hospital in Inglewood. That was back in 1966. She'd be a teen-ager now, so I wasn't sure if you were still interested. I can't imagine what the ESP angle could be."

Enders paused, with his fork halfway to his mouth. He set the fork down on his plate.

"Yes, I know that case, I'm definitely interested."

"Yeah, well, George, it was flagged "Contact CIA" with the notation ESP with a question mark. What's that got to do with a missing baby?"

"Maybe nothing, but some of the witnesses interviewed about the kidnapping indicated concern that the child was somehow communicating with them mentally."

"I'm getting goose bumps." Kent said, smiling.

"Okay, Howard, what has happened to bring the case up again?"

Kent handed him the police report. "I made a copy for you. The short story is that a P.I. had an appointment to interview a nurse. She had been working at the hospital during the abduction. When he arrived, he found the nurse had been tortured and murdered. He called our Harbor division and reported the crime. She had been dead several hours so they cleared him and cut him loose."

"Do you know what he wanted to talk to the victim about?"

"He told the investigating police detective that he had been hired to find the missing girl. The nurse was one of his leads."

"Does the report state who he was hired by?"

"No, but this is probably an abbreviated report. Ernesto Chavez was the investigating detective and may have more information."

"Damn, Chavez is a hard ass. He's not going to tell me anything. May I keep this?"

"It's yours. Just don't let anyone know I gave it to you."

Enders folded the report and put it into an inside coat pocket. "No one else knows about this, right?"

"Only the two of us, what do you think, any money in this for us? I'm trying to beef up my retirement stash."

"Yeah, me too, I'll let you know." They finished their meals and left.

TWENTY FOUR

"Are you my daddy?" she kept asking. It was the first thing in my mind when I woke. *Why can't I get that kid out of my mind?*

I saw it was getting late and realized that I was getting hungry. I decided to find someplace to eat. I dressed and walked out to Highland where I spotted a diner about a block down the street. After eating I headed back toward my room. The sun had set, and now, except for the moonlight, it was dark. The street was lit by antique lamp posts. Sounds of the surf behind my room were enticing.

I walked down the hand railed steps to the strand. It is an approximate twelve foot wide paved walkway which stretches both ways as far as one can see. It was deserted this time of day, except for a few pedestrians. The strand is illuminated by the same picturesque type lamps as the street. During the day it's used by walkers, joggers, skaters, skateboarders and bicyclists.

I sat on a bench watching the waves roll in. The half-moon enhanced the fluorescent sparkle of minerals in the surf. The ocean sound drowned out street noise and conversation from people walking by behind me. I watched ship lights on the horizon moving in both directions and jet liners taking off from LAX. I took a deep breath, taking in the salty sea air.

Where are those ships going? I wondered. *Maybe San Francisco or Alaska, or they could be heading for South America, the Panama Canal or Hawaii.* It was awe inspiring to be sitting on the edge of the continent with the rest of the world out there.

All right, I thought, *tomorrow I'll go to San Pedro and see Rosie Flores. So far I'm not much closer to finding the girl. Rosie is my last lead unless she can point me to someone else. There also is the nurse Ann or Annie, last name unknown, and the lady doctor, Janet Gresso, address unknown. I've got to find the girl before Harding. I don't know why he wants her, but it can't be good for her.*

I leaned back and closed my eyes listening to the soothing roar of the surf. I was drifting off when a helicopter cruising along the beach swooped low as it passed. The whine of the engine and rotor snapped me awake. I quickly oriented myself, *relax Jake, you're not in Vietnam anymore.* The chopper moved on down the beach, lights blinking, finally disappearing. I felt a few raindrops hit my face. The light rain felt good for a few minutes until it started pelting down. I finally stood and headed up the steps to my room.

The next morning, I had breakfast and headed for San Pedro. I went south on Highland to Rosecrans and east to the 405 freeway. Then I drove south to the Harbor freeway and down to San Pedro. I had finally worked up the courage to drive the freeways. I had the unrealistic feeling that the other drivers knew I was a novice and were keeping a wary eye on me.

TWENTY FIVE

George Enders parked in the Savoir Regent ground level parking lot and walked around to the front entrance. He badged the clerk behind the front desk.

"I'm looking for Jacob Canoe. Is he in his room?"

"Not any more, he checked out."

"What's your name, son?"

"I'm Jeff."

"Okay Jeff, when did he leave?"

"I think it was sometime yesterday."

"Do you know where he went?"

"Hey, nobody tells me where they're going, they just go."

"Is it okay to look at his room?"

"Knock yourself out, it's empty and already been cleaned."

Jeff tossed the key on the counter. "It's Room 615. Take the elevator up to six, three doors to the left."

Enders let himself in and visually scanned the room. He went to the bathroom and checked the medicine cabinet and waste basket. He opened the closet door and looked inside, reaching up on the shelf. After searching the bedroom and kitchen, he decided the kid was right, there was nothing here. He locked the door and headed back to the lobby.

"Did you see him leave?" Enders asked.

"No, I was dealing with another guest."

"Did he go out the front or into the garage?"

"I think he might have gone out the front."

"Did you see anyone pick him up or did he get into a taxi?"

"Sorry, like I said, I didn't see what he did."

"Okay, thanks," Enders answered.

A few minutes later, Enders was back in his car. *That was a waste of time.* He sat for a few minutes to plan his next move. *Maybe he left town, went back to Wichita.* He headed to the airport.

Enders parked in a red zone and climbed out. An airport cop was disgustedly shaking his head as he swaggered toward the car. Enders watched the cop hitch up his pants and try to stand a little taller as he approached.

Before the cop could speak, Enders showed his badge and ID.

"Official business, watch my car for me, if I get towed your ass is mine."

"Yes sir," the cop answered, losing the attitude.

"Anything I can help you with?"

Enders ignored him and walked into the terminal and went to a counter.

Showing the female attendant his badge he said, "I need to know if a certain person flew out of here in the last forty-eight hours."

"What's the name?"

Twenty Five

"Jacob Canoe, he might be flying to Wichita."

Enders waited while she pecked away on her computer.

"I see he arrived a week ago," she answered, "But hasn't taken a flight out to anywhere. I'd say he's still in town unless he drove, took a bus or train."

"All right, thank you," Enders said, turning away.

"Wait," she said, "According to what it says here, he rented a car yesterday, try the Hertz lot across the street."

Enders went out and saw the cop dutifully watching his car. Enders waved and pointed across the street. The cop nodded back. Enders took the crosswalk with a mob of travelers and walked to the Hertz rental office. He identified himself and asked to see the rental agreement for Canoe's car.

The attendant thumbed through a file cabinet and pulled out a sheet of paper and set it on the counter.

Enders jotted down the car description and plate number along with the address Canoe was staying at. He hiked back across the street for his car and headed for El Segundo.

Twenty minutes later, Enders parked in front of the motel office, and went into the manager's office. A man was perched on a stool behind the counter.

"Where's Jacob Canoe's room?" Enders asked.

"It's across over there, in the rear," the manager answered, pointing.

"Where's his car?"

"He's not here, he's been gone since this morning."

"Are you sure?"

"I wouldn't be much of a manager if I didn't know what was going on around here."

"Do you have a key to his room?"

"You ain't getting it if I do."

Enders pulled his badge out and showed Andy his ID.

"Official business," he said.

"That badge don't mean shit to me, my nephew got one just like it for three bucks at Knott's Berry Farm. He even got a secret de-coder ring."

Enders bristled, "It would behoove you, sir, to cooperate with a government agency."

"Absolutely sir, I'll be glad to, where's your search warrant?"

"Who do you think you are? Some damned lawyer?"

Enders looked around, "I don't see a degree on the wall."

"Those are my degrees," Andy said, pointing behind him, I know the law."

Enders looked at the framed military medals and honorable discharge certificate.

"Okay, you got me. I just need a quick look. You can go in with me."

"A quick look, my ass, Mister Canoe's got rights, and you ain't getting in without a warrant."

"Here's my card, call me if he shows up."

Enders tossed the card on the counter and stormed out the door. He jumped in his car, started it and peeled out with tires squealing.

"Ain't no damn pencil pushing bureaucrat gonna shove me around." The manager muttered as he watched Enders drive off.

Twenty Five

Enders pulled over two blocks down the road to cool off. *Okay,* he thought, *let's see, what's my next move?* A few minutes later he headed back to the airport. He drove directly to the car rental office. The same attendant was at the front desk. He showed her his badge again.

She smiled, "Yes sir, I remember you."

"I read an article in Mechanics Illustrated that some car rentals firms are installing some kind of tracking device in vehicles. Do you have any way to track the location of your rentals?"

She paused, "Just a minute, sir."

She went to a phone, talked for a couple minutes and then returned to the counter. She pointed toward an office.

"Go in there and talk to our manager."

―――※―――

Jamie woke with a start when she heard the rap on her bedroom door.

"Jamie, it's time to get up for school. I'll start your oatmeal."

"Okay Mom, thanks, I'll be there in a few minutes."

She had the same dream again. An old Indian man with long white hair was talking to her. She thought he was Indian from his appearance and voice. He spoke in a soft, soothing voice and was in no way frightening. She lay staring at the ceiling, trying to remember his exact words.

"Don't worry," the voice said, "He will find and protect you."

"Who will protect me?" Jamie asked in her dream.

"The warrior," the Indian said.

The Indian turned and looked back over his shoulder. She could see a shadowy figure behind him. The face was slightly out of focus and the only feature she could make out was a line or scar on his cheek. The dream would then fade away, but was crystal clear when she woke.

"Your breakfast is almost done," her mom yelled.

"All right, I'm coming right now," she yelled back.

TWENTY SIX

San Pedro is the official port of Los Angeles and is adjacent to the US Navy shipyards. The Queen Mary is also docked in San Pedro as a tourist attraction. The terrain, for the most part, is hilly with narrow streets lined with white washed, red tile roofed houses. Several generations of Portuguese and Italian dockworkers have lived and worked in San Pedro for a century. It is not unusual to find an entire family of men working the docks. The harbor is a busy place with commercial shipping along with fishing and recreational boats cruising in and out twenty four hours a day.

I parked at the curb in front of Rosie's house. There was a car parked at the top of the driveway so I started walking up to the door.

"Are you looking for Rosie?" a voice asked.

I turned and saw a woman weeding a flower bed next door.

"Yes, I am."

"She's in the hospital."

This doesn't sound good, I thought, walking over to the fence.

"What happened to her?" I asked.

The woman stood and walked over to me. She was wearing a big floppy hat with a wide brim. She raised her head to look at me and squinted against the sun.

"Her daughter came by like she does every morning. I think it was about seven. Someone had broken in during the night and beat the old lady up. The police just left, they said it must have been a robbery."

She shook her head. "This has always been a safe neighborhood."

"I'm a private investigator. I had an appointment with her at ten. Is she going to be all right?"

"They don't know, the last I heard, she's in a coma. Her daughter would be the best person to talk to, but she might still be at the hospital. I could try calling her house. It's only a few blocks from here"

"Thank you, I appreciate that." I said.

I waited while the woman went inside to make the call.

A few minutes later she came out. "She just got back to her house and says she'd like to talk to you. She's leaving now and will be here shortly."

Minutes later a Jeep CJ-5 pulled in behind my car. An attractive woman approached me with a puzzled look. I sized her up. *She was fit, suntanned, no nonsense and damn good looking.*

"Hi, I'm Tina, why were you coming to see my mom?" she demanded.

I gave her a card and showed my I.D.

"I'm Jacob Canoe. I wanted to talk to her about a baby that went missing when your mother was a nurse. I've been hired to re-investigate the case. Gladys Crain called your mother yesterday. She said it was okay for me to come over"

"I remember the baby kidnapping when mom was at Daniel Freeman, it was a big to-do for a few weeks. How could my mom help you?"

Twenty Six

"I wanted to ask what recollections she had about the abduction. Any nurse's names that I don't already have on my list, or any suspicions of what happened to the child."

"I'm sorry. I don't know how I can help you now."
"What was stolen from the house?"
"That's the funny thing. I looked through the house thoroughly and can't find anything missing."
"Do you know a nurse named Ann or Annie, a nurse your mother worked with?"
"The name sounds familiar, I remember my mom talking about her, but I don't know her."
"Do you recall her last name?"
"No, but maybe it's in my mom's little black book. She keeps it next to the phone. She's had the note book for years and it's stuffed with numbers and addresses. Come in with me, we'll look for it." She had warmed up a little.

I followed her in the back door and into the kitchen. Tina looked on the counter under the wall phone. When she didn't see it she pulled out a few drawers but still couldn't find the book. She looked around the room with a puzzled expression.

"Oh, I know, it's probably on her bedside table, she has a phone there."

She came back, but with no little black book.
"That's strange, where could she have put it?"
Tina stood with her hands on her hips and surveyed the kitchen again, then walked to the doorway to the living room and looked in there. She turned back and shrugged.

Thoughts were spinning in my head. *Whoever broke in must have taken it. This smells like more of Harding's work. How in the hell did he get here before me?*

"Wait a minute," Tina said, her face brightening, "Maybe it's in her car. I'll be right back."

A minute later she ran back in the door with a big smile. "Here it is. It was on the front seat."

She handed it to me, and I opened it to the "G" page. There were three entries, the first was Annie Gilchrist. There was a phone number but no address.

Bingo, this has to be it. I thought. *I hope Harding or Cecil wasn't here and got the address from Rosie. Maybe it wasn't them that broke in and assaulted her, but I'm starting to lose faith in maybe.*

"Did you find what you were looking for?" Tina asked.

"Yeah, I did, it's a long shot that she can help me find the missing girl, but I'm running out of leads. She's my last hope."

I wrote the name and phone number in my notebook.

Tina took two bottles of beer from the refrigerator and set them on the table. After rummaging around in a drawer she pulled out a bottle opener.

"Have a seat", she motioned to the kitchen table and chairs.

I sat down. She opened the beers and sat across from me. We both took a swallow. She was studying the card I gave her.

"I see that your detective agency is in Wichita. Why are you working a case in California?"

"Our firm was hired by an L.A. attorney, name of Baxter Harding. He claimed the missing girl's grandfather was looking for her. I'm sure that's a lie, but I don't know why he's really trying to find her."

"But why did he hire you from another state?"

"We have a reputation of being able to find the un-findable."

"Hmm, I see," she said, taking a sip of her beer.

"May I use the phone?" I asked.

"Sure, go ahead."

I dialed the number for Ann Gilchrist. I got a recording stating that the number was no longer in service.

"It looks like I'm back to square one, the Gilchrist phone number is no good, and there's no address in your mother's book. Is it all right if I call someone else?"

"Be my guest," she said.

I opened my note pad, found Gladys's number and dialed her. An ominous feeling crept over me after a few rings, but then I heard a weak voice answer.

"Hello, this is Gladys."

"Gladys, this is Jake, are you okay?"

"Yes Jake, I had to tell them everything I told you."

"That's all right Gladys, you did the right thing, I'm sorry I got you into this."

"Don't worry about me Jake, I'll survive."

"What did they look like?"

"The tall one with the goatee was the mean one."

Cecil, I thought, "All right Gladys, again, I'm sorry I got you into this."

"Uh Jake…maybe you shouldn't come back."

"I won't, but I'm sure they'll not be returning, they've moved on to other victims."

"Goodbye, Jake," Gladys said and hung up.

Tina was studying my face, "Do you think the people looking for the baby, are responsible for hurting my mother?"

"I'm sure of it," I answered, taking another swallow of beer.

She was staring at my face, then reached over and traced a fingernail down my scar.

"Ouch, that must have hurt a little," she said.

Her touch made me shiver and get goose bumps, "Yeah, a little," I answered.

She smiled at my reaction, "The scar gives your face character."

"Yeah, I know. My face had no character at all until it got slashed open. Every time I look in the mirror, it makes me feel good."

"Uh oh, I've offended you." She said, teasingly.

"No you haven't, Tina," I said, laughing, "I would be more offended if you tried to ignore it."

She leaned over and kissed me on the cheek, "Does that make you feel better?"

"Now you're trying to butter me up... and it's working," I said.

We each had another pull on our beers. I felt like an idiot, I couldn't quit grinning at her.

"Should we call the police about all this?" she asked.

"The police quit looking for the girl years ago when they couldn't find her after a month. We don't have anything solid to tell them, and can't prove who hurt your mother. When I find the people responsible for hurting her we'll call the police. Or I might take care of them myself."

"Do you know who they are?"

"I'm convinced that they're Harding's crew, but I don't have anything to go to the police with."

"What are you going to do next?"

"I was going to go see Annie Gilchrist, but all I have is a worthless phone number."

I took another sip of beer and paused, a thought hit me. I reached into my jacket pocket and pulled out the note book from the suitcase in Hollywood.

I started thumbing through it and found the G's, no luck, no entry for Gilchrist. I thought for a few seconds and went to the A's. Sure enough, there it was, Annie, no last name, with an address in Venice and the same phone number in Rosie's book.

"Okay, now I have an address, a place named Venice. Do you know where that is?"

"Yes, let me go with you. I want to be there when you find whoever hurt my mother."

"I don't think so, it could get dangerous."

"I can take care of myself and I'll stay out of your way."

"Don't you have a family?"

"No, it's just me and my mom." she answered.

Maybe she would be a help to me, I thought, or *is that only an excuse to take her with me?*

"Please," she asked, staring at me with her big brown eyes.

I knew I was hooked and she knew it too.

She smiled, "Follow me to my place, so I can drop off my Jeep."

I tailed her the two blocks, "I'll be right out," she said, running into her house.

Ten minutes later, when she came out, my heartbeat picked up a notch. She was wearing tight jeans with boots. She had put on a gray tee shirt with a red nylon wind breaker. She was wearing a khaki cap with the letters USMC above the bill. When she bent down to get in, I saw a holster with gun butt showing under the jacket.

"I called the hospital, they say my mom's still in a coma but holding her own. I offered to come back, but they said there's nothing I can do. I just have to keep checking in."

"Don't tell me you're a jar-head?"

"Damn straight and proud of it."

"What did you do in the corps? Women aren't allowed in combat."

"I was in the military police, two years in HASP, and then finished up in Sasebo, Japan, at the navy base."

"What's HASP?" I asked.

"Hawaii Armed Services Police, mostly I was picking up drunks. In Sasebo I did everything from gate duty to hauling AWOL's out of cat houses."

"What do you do now?"

"Security and investigator, I work for the L.A. Port Authority."

"Do you have a license for that?" I asked, nodding at the gun.

"Of course," she answered.

"Are you familiar with the city of Venice?" I asked.

"Well, somewhat, it's got a nice beach and little canals like Venice, Italy."

"Okay, grab that map book off the back seat and look up the Gilchrist address while we're on the way."

TWENTY SEVEN

Enders entered the car rental manager's office. The man sitting at the desk motioned toward a chair.

"Have a seat Agent Enders. May I see your identification?"

Enders set his I.D. on the desk. The man inspected the badge and compared the photo to the man sitting in front of him. He opened a drawer, pulled out a form and slid it to Enders, "Fill this out."

"What is it?"

"It's a non-disclosure for what I'm about to tell you."

Enders filled out the form and handed it back.

"Agent Enders, we do have an experimental program for tracking some of our vehicles. We hope to have the kinks worked out and fully operational in another two years. It's not foolproof and works best when the target vehicle is parked. The particular car you asked about is moving at this time, on the harbor freeway heading north."

"I would like to know when and where it's parked for any length of time." Enders said.

"We can do that. I'll call you when we've got something."

The brakes squealed as the school bus came to a stop at the corner. A few kids headed down the aisle to get off. Jamie put the book she was reading into her backpack and zipped it closed. She stood and was the last to get off the bus.

"Good bye Missus Busch", Jamie said to the driver as she stepped down onto the sidewalk.

"See you tomorrow, Jamie."

She heard the bus door close behind her as she stepped on the sidewalk.

As she neared the house her antennae momentarily went up at the sight of an unfamiliar van parked at the curb. She had never seen that vehicle in the neighborhood. The uneasy feeling subsided somewhat when she saw her mother's car in the driveway. *It's probably someone visiting one of the other houses.* She thought.

She unlocked the door and entered the dark front room. Down the hall she could see the kitchen light was on.

"Mom," she yelled, "I'm home." There was no answer so she headed toward the kitchen.

She stopped when she smelled cigarette smoke.

"Mom, are you here?"

There was still no answer so she cautiously walked into the kitchen. She froze when she saw two men sitting at the table.

Twenty Seven

"Take it easy, Jamie, don't do anything crazy, your mom is okay."

"Where is she? What have you done with her?"

"I don't know where she is. She went with some really bad men, but will be perfectly safe as long as you cooperate. Her location is unknown, even to us. There's no use trying to read our minds."

"Read your minds, are you crazy?"

"I wouldn't expect any other response, Jamie. We're not the ones you have to convince. It's those bad men that are with your mother that want your cooperation. We are going to ask you to go with us."

"I want to talk with my mom, call her on the phone or I'm not going anywhere."

Cecil reached for the wall phone. He smiled at Jamie while he dialed.

"Of course, Jamie, we want you to talk to your mother so you'll know how serious we are."

"My mom doesn't allow smoking in the house."

Cecil dropped the butt on the linoleum floor and ground it out with the sole of his shoe.

"You're a pig," Jamie said.

Cecil ignored her and spoke into the phone, "She wants to talk to her mother."

Jamie grabbed the phone when he handed it to her.

"Mom, are you all right, where are you?"

A man's voice answered. "Hello, Jamie, I want you to listen to something before you talk to your mother."

Jamie put the phone to her ear and heard a series of screams which turned to anguished sobs.

"Mom, is that you? What are they doing?"

Jamie's mother finally answered between gasps. She sounded out of breath.

"Jamie, please do what they tell you."

"Okay Mom, I love you, I'll do what they say."

Cecil snatched the phone from her and hung it up.

"What are they doing to her?" Jamie asked.

"It'll get worse if you give us any trouble." Cecil said.

"Okay, let's get her in the van," he said to the man sitting at the table.

"I gotta hit the john, I'll be right behind you," the man said.

Cecil took hold of Jamie's arm and began leading her to the front door.

―――――

We parked at the curb across the street from Ann Gilchrist's house. I saw a car in the driveway and a van parked on the street in front.

"Leave your gun in the car, I don't think you're going to need it," I said.

Tina reluctantly un-clipped the holster from her belt and shoved it under her seat. We walked up to the front door. I lifted my hand to knock when the door suddenly opened. Cecil had a stunned look on his face when he saw me standing in front of him. He let go of the girl's arm and took a step backward.

When I hit him, Cecil staggered back into the room.

"That's for Mildred Lerch," I said.

Tina sized up the situation and immediately gave Cecil a spin kick to the chest. He fell back onto the kitchen floor.

"And that's for my mother," she yelled.

I didn't see or hear the other man come out of a side hall. The last thing I heard was Tina or the girl let out a scream, then blinding pain and darkness.

When I woke I realized my right wrist was handcuffed to a bracket on the van wall. I reached with my other hand and felt a tender lump behind my ear. When I checked my fingers for blood, there wasn't any. Tina and the girl were both looking at me. Tina also had a handcuffed wrist.

"Are you all right?" Tina asked.

"Yeah, I think so, but I feel sick." I answered.

The swaying of the van and my throbbing head was making me feel nauseated. I dry heaved a couple times then leaned over and puked in the rear corner of the van floor.

"Sorry about that, how long was I out?" I asked.

"No more than five minutes," Tina answered.

Jamie was mystified by all that was going on.

"Who are you?" she asked me.

"My name's Jacob Canoe, this is Tina."

"We've met," the girl said.

"I'm a detective looking for a lost girl. I thought that you were her."

"I'm not lost, just kidnapped by those guys," she said, nodding at Cecil and the other goon in the front seat.

"Yeah, I can see that."

"They took my mom. They'll hurt her if I don't do what they want."

"What is it they want you to do?" Tina asked.

"I don't know, but they seem to think I can read their minds."

"What! That's crazy," Tina said.

"That's what I told them," Jamie answered.

I didn't say anything. I'm sure this is the kidnapped girl and had heard about her possible ESP from almost everyone I questioned, but I still wasn't convinced. The girl was denying it but Harding's crew may believe it. That could be their motivation for snatching the girl.

"What's your name?" Tina asked the girl.

"My name's Jamie Gilchrist."

I saw the girl staring at me in the semi-darkness of the van.

"Is that a scar on your cheek?" she asked.

"Yes, it is," I answered, wondering why she asked.

"This may sound strange, but, are you the warrior?"

I was taken aback. "Only one person ever called me that. That was years ago when I was a kid."

"Was he an Indian with long white hair?"

When she asked that, the hair stood up on the back of my neck.

I was so amazed I could hardly speak. "How could you know that?" I asked.

"I keep having dreams with the Indian talking to me," she answered.

Tina was watching my conversation with Jamie. She had a puzzled look on her face.

Suddenly the van slowed, turned a corner and stopped. We sat with the engine idling for a few seconds when I heard another vehicle pull up next to us.

"They're here," Cecil said as he got out the passenger door.

The side door was rolled back and Cecil was standing in front of the open door. A passenger car was parked next to them with a man behind the wheel. Another man walked around and took Cecil's place in the van.

Twenty Seven

"We're taking the girl with us. You take these two out to the farm." Cecil told the two men.

"Do you want us to make them disappear?"

"No, lock them in the barn. I want to deal with them myself, later." Cecil leered at Tina.

Jamie began struggling when Cecil pulled her from the van.

"No, I want to stay with them," she yelled.

He backhanded her and shoved her into the back seat.

"We'll find you Jamie," Tina yelled, then added to Cecil, "We'll find you too, asshole, you're going to pay for that."

I wish I had her optimism, I thought, *but at least we have more time to figure a way out.* I was still stunned by what the girl said about an Indian. Sam, my mentor, always called me "Little Warrior," when I was a kid.

We drove more than an hour when the van slowed and turned onto a bumpy road which, from the sound, I thought must be dirt. The van bounced along, and then I heard the tires, bleep… bleep… bleep, over what felt like a cattle guard. We continued on the dirt road until they made a left turn, slowed to a stop and the motor was turned off. The two goons got out and the side door slid open. One held a gun on us while the other unlocked the hand cuffs.

The one with the gun waved us out of the van and motioned toward a large metal barn. I looked around and saw a house, with a big front porch, about twenty yards away. The driveway we drove in on was about forty yards long ending at the dirt road. A freshly plowed field was on the other side of the road. I couldn't see any other houses or structures, only flat farmland. I could hear some highway traffic noise from the way we came.

The barn had a large lift up vehicle door with a smaller hinged pedestrian door in the center. We were herded through the smaller door. When we were in, we heard the door being padlocked from the outside.

Tina sat on a hay bale rubbing her wrist where the handcuff had chafed it, while I wandered the inside perimeter.

We could hear the two men talking in low voices, and then one said loudly, "C'mon let's go in the house and grab some beers."

"Yeah, they're not going anywhere," the other one answered.

"Are you all right?" Tina asked.

"Yes, I think so, just a headache."

"What was she talking about? You know, an Indian in her dreams."

"I'm not sure, I hope we get a chance to ask, but we've got a bigger problem now."

Tina went to the door and looked out the crack around it.

"The van's still parked out there, but I don't see them."

She moved to a side wall and found a hole she could see out through.

"They're heading for the house."

She paused, "They're on the porch," another pause, "Okay, now they're in the house."

I looked around and saw two windows high up on each side. They were too small to get out of even if they could be reached. The sun hadn't set yet so I had plenty of light to check out our surroundings.

"How are we going to get out of here?" Tina asked.

"I'm thinking on it," I answered.

I took visible inventory and saw an extension ladder leaning on a wall. Hooks on the wall held coils of bailing wire and rope. There was an old four cylinder engine from a tractor or truck sitting along one wall. I

Twenty Seven

walked around looking for a sledge hammer or some tool I could use to get the door open. There was nothing. I went to the door and hit it with my shoulder a few times but it didn't budge. *Now I see why they didn't bother to tie or chain us up in here.*

I looked up and saw a track supported with brackets extending from one end of the barn to the other. It was about ten feet from the floor. A hoist motor with chain and hook was hanging from the track. I saw an electrical conduit loosely hanging from the motor. The wiring looped over to a wall bracket and down the wall to a switch panel. The panel had six push buttons, a red and white one on top with four black buttons mounted underneath.

I pushed the red button and heard the motor start up. I pushed the white button and it stopped running. I restarted the motor and pushed one of the black buttons and the hoist started moving on the track toward the rear of the barn. When I released it the hoist stopped moving.

After a little more experimenting I mastered the function of the other buttons. I could move the hoist back and forth and lower or raise the chain and hook.

"Can you see them anywhere out there?" I asked.

Tina peered out the hole again, "No, they must still be in the house. I can hear music or a TV."

I sat down again and kept eyeing the hoist.

Tina was staring at me, "Have you got something figured out?"

"Maybe," I answered. I returned to the control panel, started the motor and moved the hoist to the door end and lowered the chain. I hooked the chain to the door and moved the hoist back a few feet. When the chain went taut the motor bogged down and was humming louder.

I released the button, *that's no good,* I thought, *the door frame is too strong and I don't want to burn out the motor or trip a circuit breaker.* I moved the motor forward to relieve the strain and unhooked the chain. I sat back down to study the situation. Looking around, my eyes fell on the old engine.

I sat thinking for a few minutes when something occurred to me. I jumped up and went to the control panel. I moved the hoist motor down the rails until it was directly across from the engine. I lowered the chain to its full length where it piled up on the ground under the hoist. I attached the hook to the engine and used the control to pull the chain up.

When the chain went taut the engine began to drag along the dirt floor of the barn until it was directly under the hoist motor. I raised the engine until it was about three feet off the ground, and then moved it toward the door. I tried shoving the engine into the door but only succeeded in making dents.

"Is anyone coming from the house?" I asked.

"No, I think they have the music too loud to hear anything."

I went back to thinking again. *I need to get the motor higher so it will swing down with more force.*

I spotted the heavy rope hanging on a hook.

"I've got another idea," I said to Tina, taking the coil of rope from the wall.

I used the control to move the engine back about ten feet. I placed the extension ladder under the hoist track and leaned it on the track behind the hoist motor. I then tied one end of the rope to the engine and went up the ladder with the other end. I pulled the slack out of the rope and tied it to a track brace with a slip knot. I went back to the motor

Twenty Seven

control and slowly moved the engine toward the door. As the hoist closed the distance to the door the rope tightened and the engine began lifting up.

It looks like I estimated the distance okay. I hope the rope and slip knot hold. I thought.

I stopped the motor about three feet from the door. The engine was suspended about six to seven feet off the floor. The rope and slip knot were holding.

"Tina, we've got only one chance, I want you to start yelling and banging on the big door to get their attention. Don't get between the engine and the small door."

Tina started hammering on the aluminum wall and yelling, like I told her. She would pause long enough for a quick peek out the hole and then start with the noise again.

"Here they come, they must have heard me," she yelled.

I went up the ladder, "Keep making noise, and tell me when they're in front of the door."

"They're almost here."

I heard the men yelling and threatening us to shut up.

"They're right in front of the door," Tina yelled, giving the door one last bang.

"Get back," I yelled as I yanked on the loose end of the slip knot. It didn't pull loose so I gave another hard pull and felt it give. The engine swung like a pendulum, crashed through the pedestrian door, ripping it off the hinges.

Tina was still standing to one side. I got to the door just as the engine was on its backward swing. I jumped back as it went by and waited for it to swing forward again. When it did, I slipped through the erupted door and ran outside with Tina behind me.

The two men were on the ground. One had a smashed face, with blank eyes staring at the sky. He was obviously dead. The other had a caved in chest with a two inch hole where an engine part had punched into him. We watched blood pump out the hole until after a couple of spasmodic spurts the blood was reduced to a slow flow and then stopped.

"Are the keys in the van?" I asked.

Tina ran to the van and looked in, "Yes, they are."

"Okay, let's get out of here."

It was almost dark, but there was enough light to drive without the headlamps on. We headed down the dirt road toward the highway, drove over the cattle guard and stopped at the paved road.

"I think we came from that way," I said, pointing to the left.

"Yeah, me too," Tina answered.

Ten miles down the road we came to an intersection with a gas station, diner and small motel. The sun had set and it was now dark.

"Let's get something to eat," I said.

"Good idea," Tina said, "I'm famished."

I circled the diner and parked in the rear. We walked around to the front door where I had a good view through the windows. There were about ten cars parked in front and the patrons inside appeared to be families or couples. Nothing set off alarms so we went in and were greeted by a waitress.

"Hi, folks, would you like a table or booth?"

"We'll have a window booth."

"Take your choice, would you like coffee?"

"Yes, please, cream and sugar." Tina answered.

Twenty Seven

The waitress brought the coffee and menus. We ordered food and sipped our coffee until the meals arrived.

"Okay, what's next?" Tina asked.

"We need to get back to town for our car before we can do anything. Now that Harding and his crew have Jamie, we'll have to find where they're holding her. When we find them we'll find Jamie."

After eating, I called the waitress over, "We're not from around here and are a little lost. How far are we from L.A.?"

"Well, you're in Riverside County so it depends where in L.A. you want to go."

"Tell me exactly where we are, we may have somebody come pick us up."

The waitress went to the counter and returned with a restaurant business card. I glanced at it and shoved it into my shirt pocket.

"Let's stay the night in the motel, I'm going to have someone pick us up in the morning and get us back to my car. We'll wipe down the van and dump it here or nearby. I don't want to get stopped in someone else's vehicle. We definitely don't want to be connected to two dead men."

"Sounds like a plan, you get the couch," Tina said.

"I wouldn't have it any other way," I answered.

I paid the check, drove the van from behind the restaurant, and parked it in a space back of the motel, where it couldn't be seen from the road.

"I'm going to use the pay phone, you get us checked in, false names, of course," I said.

"Of course," she answered.

I took out my wallet and dug through for the business card I was looking for. I dropped in some coins and dialed.

I heard Sid answer; "Ajax Detective agency."

"Hello Sid, don't you ever go home?"

"Is that you, Jacob?"

"Yeah, Sid, it's me. I need your services tomorrow morning. Are you going to be available?"

"I'll make an exception for you Jake. What's the deal?"

"We're at a motel in Riverside County. The café business card reads *Brea Junction*. Do you know where it is?"

"Oh sure, I can drive right to it. You said we?"

"Yeah, there are two of us, and we need a ride to my car in Venice."

"How the hell did you get so far from your car?"

"It's a long story Sid, I'll tell you about it tomorrow."

"How about nine o'clock?"

"All right, Sid, see you then."

I hung up, turned and saw Tina heading my way. She was smiling and swinging the motel key back and forth between two fingers.

TWENTY EIGHT

Cecil pulled into the farm driveway the next morning. He stopped near the two bodies, frightening away birds scavenging the remains. Harding and Cecil sat for a minute staring at the destroyed barn door and the bodies.

"What the hell?" Cecil said.

Harding didn't say anything.

They climbed out of the car, walked to the barn and looked at the engine hanging from the hoist, and back at the bodies. The birds had lined up on a wooden fence, shifting around, waiting to get back to their meal.

"That Canoe is one ingenious bastard. I see how he did it." Harding said.

"I guess the Chicago guys weren't as smart as we thought." Cecil said.

"You used poor judgment, Cecil. You should have killed them both when you had the chance."

"Yes sir, I know, Mister Harding."

"There are times, Cecil, when your sadistic proclivities interfere with your common sense."

"I'm sorry, Mister Harding."

"Okay Cecil, get a shovel out of the barn and start digging. I'm going into the house to make a phone call, we need more muscle."

Tina tossed a pillow and blanket on the couch for me. I was exhausted and felt my eyes closing within in seconds of stretching out.

I am standing at the fork in the path. Behind me is a solid, impenetrable, green wall of trees. The path to the right is drawing me like a magnet and I can't resist taking it. There is no choice. I have to take that path. I know that something is waiting there for me, but I do not feel any fear. It is a mission or task that only I can do.

Now I can see a clearing ahead with something in the middle of the space. The object begins to take shape as I get near. Now I'm in the clearing and starting to get a sick feeling in my stomach when the object begins to look familiar. When I recognize the object, for what it is, a brief flash of panic floods over me. I reach for my rifle and when I realize I don't have it, I reach for my K-BAR knife. I have neither. The object is a large bamboo cage, lashed together with strips of peeled bark. NO, NO, I won't go in there again. Then I see something move inside the cage but I can't make out the features. The door is tied shut and it can't get out.

"Jake, are you all right?" I heard Tina asking.

I was sitting upright.

"Yeah, I'm okay, just a dream."

Twenty Eight

"You're soaked with sweat. It must have been a bad dream."

"I guess it was, I'm going to take a shower, you go back to sleep."

After a cold shower, I hit the couch again, fell asleep immediately and slept soundly the rest of the night.

The next morning we finished breakfast and were waiting for Sid when he pulled in. I had already parked the van in the rear of the café lot. I left the doors unlocked with the key in the ignition and spent fifteen minutes wiping it down. We piled into Sid's car with Tina getting in the back seat. I made the introductions and we took off for Venice.

"Okay Jake, what's going on?" Sid asked.

"You were right when you warned me about Harding. He got to the girl I was looking for before I did. Two of his crew brought us out here on a one way trip."

"What happened to them?"

"You don't want to know, I imagine they're starting to smell pretty bad by now."

"Do you think she really is the girl kidnapped from the hospital?"

"I think she could be, but they definitely think she is."

"I've got some other interesting news for you, Jake."

"What's that?"

"You asked me to check out Doctor Janet Gresso, well, she doesn't exist anymore."

"She doesn't exist?"

"Yeah, she got married about eight years ago, and has a new name."

"Don't tease me, Sid."

"Her name now is Missus Baxter Harding."

I shook my head. "The twists in this case just keep coming. I'm convinced that there is no grandfather. They want the girl for some other reason. Well, now I know that Janet Gresso didn't kidnap the baby."

They were waiting in the bank parking lot. Cecil said to Jamie, "We're going to do this just like we rehearsed, if anything goes wrong, someone's going to die."

"I'll try, but I can't promise I can do what you want."

"Sure you can, just keep thinking of your mother."

A few minutes later they watched a woman exit the bank. She had a purse slung over one shoulder and was carrying a zippered bank wallet.

Cecil looked around and saw that the lot was empty except for the woman.

"Here we go, get the bank bag from her." Cecil said.

Jamie got out of the car and nervously approached the woman. Cecil watched as they both stopped, facing each other. The woman handed the bag to Jamie, then walked on past to a car. The woman got into her car and drove away. Jamie returned to the car, with Cecil waiting, got in and handed him the bag.

"All right," he said, smiling as he unzipped the bag.

His smile turned to a frown, "Damn, only a receipt, oh well, this was a good trial run, next time it's for some real money."

He tossed the bank bag out his window as they drove away.

"I'm glad it was empty, this isn't right, that woman needs her money more than you do. You should try working for it like she does." Jamie said.

Twenty Eight

"Don't be such a sap, Jamie. You'll wise up when you get older."

"How much longer are you going to keep me doing this?"

"As soon as we make a few big scores, you and your mother will go free."

"How do you know that we won't go to the police?"

"We don't think your mother will want to do that."

Jamie hunched down in the seat, wondering why he thought that.

TWENTY NINE

When his desk phone rang at exactly 8:00 a.m., Enders grabbed it.
"Hello, this is Enders."

"Agent Enders, I'm calling from Hertz. We've got a location on the car you were inquiring about. It's been parked on a street in Venice since yesterday. I can give you a street name and approximate location, but not an exact address. You're on your own with that."

Enders rode the elevator downstairs, raced to his car in the parking lot and headed for Venice. Thirty minutes later he slowly drove down the street when he spotted Canoe's rental car. He checked the license plate number to be sure.

That's it, he thought, *I've got you now.*

Enders parked in a vacant lot across the street where he could keep an eye on the vehicle. He looked at the row of houses up and down the street. *He could be anywhere around here, maybe in one of those houses, I'll have to wait for him to show himself.*

Twenty Nine

An hour and a half after leaving Brea Junction, Sid drove us into Venice and we were nearing the Gilchrist house. I saw my rental car, still parked where I had left it. I got a brain twitch when I spotted a man leaning on the fender of a car. The stranger was about fifty feet from my car.

"Keep on driving, look straight ahead. Don't pull over." I told Sid.

"What's happening?" Tina asked.

"I may be wrong, but I think our car is staked out."

I pointed down the street. "Drop us off at that store on the corner."

Sid parked, we got out and I handed Sid some folded bills.

"Is three hundred okay?"

"Perfect, thanks Jake. Are you sure you don't need me anymore?"

"Not now, Sid, but who knows what tomorrow will bring."

With a wave of his hand, Sid drove away leaving us at a convenience store. It was a busy place with cars and pedestrians coming and going.

From half a block away we watched the man drop a cigarette butt and grind it out in the dirt. He didn't look like one of Harding's crew, but who else would he be. He was definitely scoping out my rental car.

We watched him get back into his car and slump down in the seat.

"Why don't we go to your car and see what he does? We can easily take down one man," Tina said.

"I killed two men yesterday so I would rather avoid another confrontation. Also this is practically on Ann Gilchrist's doorstep."

"Killing those two yesterday was self-defense, you had no choice."

"I know. I have a choice this time."

"Well, what are we going to do?" Tina asked.

"I'm thinking," I answered.

School kids had gathered at the corner near the man's car, and then a yellow bus pulled up blocking my view of the kids and the stranger. Thirty seconds later the bus pulled away, the kids were gone and the man was getting back out of his car. He lit up another smoke, *chain smoker, nervous, antsy,* I thought.

I've got an idea." I said to Tina.

I stepped into the corner phone booth, dropped in a quarter and dialed O.

"Please connect me to the Venice area police."

I glanced at Tina as I waited for someone to answer. She had a puzzled look on her face.

Then I heard a voice say, "Sergeant Rutledge."

"Hello Sergeant, I want to report some suspicious activity. There's a man loitering near a bus stop and he's paying particular attention to children walking by."

"Oh yeah, give me a location and we'll check it out. What does he look like?"

"Bald, sun glasses, suit, near the corner of 28th and Grayson in Venice."

"All right, I'll have a patrol car check it out, what's your name?"

"My name is ...oh no!" I yelled.

"What's going on? What happened?" the cop asked.

"He just exposed himself to a little girl." I said and hung up.

Tina shook her head and grinned. "You're a bad man, Jacob."

A few minutes later we heard a siren in the distance and after another thirty seconds I could see the patrol car lights coming down the street. The man was leaning on his fender, casually smoking and unconcerned as he

Twenty Nine

turned to look at the approaching police car. He stood up straight when the police car screeched to a stop next to him. One cop jumped out of the driver's side and grabbed the man who began struggling with him. The other cop ran around from the passenger side of the squad car and backhanded the stranger who staggered back and leaned on his car for support.

The second cop was wearing black leather gloves. *Sap gloves,* I thought, used for crowd control. Lead shot filled seams on the back extending down the fingers. To an onlooker or potential witness there was nothing ominous, no overt police brutality, only a gentle slap, but the suspect would feel like he was hit with a two by four.

We watched him struggle and could hear, from half a block away, his protests.

They slammed him over the hood and snapped on handcuffs. One of the cops frisked him and showed the gun he found. They dragged him to the car, threw him in the back seat and drove off. The whole episode took about twenty seconds.

As the cop car pulled away, the small crowd that had gathered to watch all the excitement began to dissipate.

"Okay," I said, "let's get our car and get out of here."

We rushed to the car, got in and drove away.

"Let's go to my house in San Pedro," Tina said. "Since they know this car we better stash it in my garage and we'll use mine."

"How did they find my car?" I wondered aloud.

"There's no way they could know what I'm driving, we'll take my Jeep." Tina said.

"I don't want to get you any more involved."

"I don't care, I want to help. I'll call my work and tell them that I need a few days off. I've got vacation time on the books. Besides, I got involved when they hurt my mother."

"I'll think on it. If you don't mind, let's stop by my motel room. I want to shower and change clothes. You can call the hospital from there to check on your mom."

"Who do you think the man waiting at the car was?" Tina asked.

"It must have been one of Harding's men, but I've never seen him before."

"What are we going to do next?"

"Harding can't be too hard to track down, that's the only way to find the girl."

It took thirty minutes to drive to my motel. When we pulled in the driveway, the manager, Andy, ran out and excitably waved us down.

"I thought that was you, Jake. Some bozo was here looking for you yesterday afternoon."

"What did he want?"

"He asked if you were here and if you were by yourself and what you looked like and so forth. I told him I didn't know anything about you, which I don't. He wasn't too happy about that so he showed me a badge which said CIA, but it could have been phony. He wanted to look in your room, but I told him no, not without a warrant. That pissed him off even more but he didn't push it. I got the idea he was doing a little private snooping."

"Did he say anything else?"

"No, just that he wanted to talk to you about an investigation."

"Has he been back?"

Twenty Nine

"No, that was it, but he left a card, says to call when you get back."

"What'd he look like?"

"Short, shaved head, suit and tie, sunglasses he never took off."

"Okay, Andy, thanks." I said, taking the card and handing him a twenty.

I love this town, I thought, money buys anything from information to silence.

"Oops, who did that description sound like," Tina asked, with a smile.

"Yeah, it sounds like the guy we saw getting hauled off as a child molester this morning. I don't know what he wants but we better not hang around here too long. The cops may have already cut him loose. Do you want to call the hospital about your mother?"

"Yes, thank you," Tina said, taking the phone.

I watched her dial and heard her ask about her mother.

"Okay, okay," she said a couple times, and then, "Thank you, I'll call back later."

"She's looking better, they say, she's opened her eyes a few times and is stirring. I'll call again when we get to my place."

"Do you want to take a shower?" I asked.

"Sure." Tina answered.

"Go ahead. I've got to call my boss in Wichita."

While Tina was in the shower, I sat at the table, picked up my Big Chief tablet and began to make notes. I had just started to write when a thought struck me.

"Damn," I said out loud, slamming the tablet down. *I left this tablet in my hotel room while I was out running around. Harding's crew must have gone in and found it. I should have known they would have* a key. *This tablet and the telephone bug was how they kept a step ahead of me. My carelessness led them to Tina's mother. How will I explain that to Tina?*

I dialed the office number and Beth answered.

"Hello, Beth, is he there?"

"Yes he is, Jacob, he'll be right with you."

Ten seconds later Tom was on the line.

"Hello Jake, what have you got?"

"A lot has happened since we last talked. I'm pretty sure I know who the missing girl is, but she's being held somewhere by Harding's thugs. They also are holding her mother at a different location."

"What's that all about?"

"I haven't figured it out yet, they're using the mother for some kind of leverage over the daughter."

"How'd they get to the girl before you?"

"I hoped you wouldn't ask that. The best I can come up with is that they got into my room when I wasn't there, and went through my Big Chief tablet."

"All right, Jake, be careful."

"Yeah boss, I will."

"You haven't broken many laws, have you?"

Let's see, I thought, *I committed bribery, copied confidential hospital records, committed assault and battery, phoned in a false police report and, oh yeah, I killed two men.*

"No, Tom, not many, I'll check back in a couple days." I hung up.

Twenty Nine

Cecil parked in front of the bank and turned to Jamie, "Don't do anything stupid or your mother will suffer for it. We're going to a teller and you'll work your magic to have her fill a bank bag for us."

"I don't know if I can do that." Jamie answered.

"Sure you can, don't do anything stupid. We can call your mother and let you hear her scream."

"No, please, I'll try to do it, but don't hurt my mother."

There were only a few customers in the bank. Cecil and Jamie walked to a teller who smiled when they came in. Neither said anything, Cecil watched a blank look come over the teller's face as they stood in front of her. The teller pulled a canvass bag from under the counter, opened her drawer and began filling the bag with bills. Cecil took the bag and they calmly walked out to the car.

"That wasn't so hard, was it?" Cecil asked.

"It's not right. You're making me a thief. When is this going to end? When are you going to let my mother go?"

"Soon, but first we're going to take a trip to Las Vegas for a real jackpot."

The cops apologized to Enders all the way back to his car. Enders was sure that Canoe's rental wasn't going to be there when he got back. They stopped next to his car, and as he figured, the other car was gone. He got out of the patrol car, slamming the door in frustration. He got into his car and watched the cops drive off. He started the engine, turned on the AC and lit up a smoke.

I'm going to get that son of a bitch, but now how am I going to do it?

After mulling over his problem for a few minutes he headed back to the Savoir Regent Hotel.

Jeff, the desk clerk, recognized him, "Hello Agent Enders."

"Hello, I need to know who paid the rent on Canoe's room."

"Well, I don't know…."

Enders interrupted him, "Don't give me any bullshit about a warrant. If I have to, I can get one, but I'll have this place locked down for a day. I'll make it miserable for you and all your guests. Make it easy, just give me the name."

The clerk hesitated for a few seconds, and then answered.

"All right, let me pull up the record on that room."

Enders waited while Jeff typed on the computer keyboard.

Jeff looked up, "Okay, here we go. That room was reserved by an attorney named Baxter Harding. He paid for it through his Law office."

"Thank you," Enders said, "That wasn't so hard, was it?"

THIRTY

Enders left the hotel and drove back to his office. He stopped at the reception desk, "Emma, get me the home address for a lawyer named Baxter Harding."

He entered his office, took a seat at the desk and his phone buzzed.

"Yes, Emma?"

"Here's that address you wanted, Mister Enders."

He wrote it down. "Thank you, Emma."

He smiled as he hung up the phone. *All right, Mister Harding, it's time we had a chat.*

He walked down the hall to the chief agent's office and knocked on the open door. "Hello George, what's up?"

Enders entered and sat in the chair in front of the desk. His boss looked at him expectantly.

"I've been working a lead, regarding the baby kidnapped from Daniel Freeman Hospital in 1966."

"Close the door."

The chief waited for Enders to return to his chair. "How'd you get the lead?"

"From a source on the L.A.P.D., a detective I've known for years."

"Who is he?"

"His name is Howard Kent. This is one of those under the table deals so we've got to keep it confidential. He gave me a copy of a police report. It seems that a possible witness of the original abduction was recently tortured and murdered. A private investigator found the body."

"Is the P.I. a suspect?"

"No, he's clear, he had an alibi."

"So no one knows that Kent gave you the information?"

"No, I promised we would keep it under wraps, we may have to give him a payoff for the tip."

The chief nodded, "We can do that if the information is valid."

"I trust Kent, and I've got the report."

"This is still an open kidnapping case. Does the FBI know that you're working on it?"

"As far as I know, the only other person involved is the P.I. from Wichita, Kansas and the attorney that hired him."

"Do you have names?"

"Yes, the attorney is Baxter Harding, a real sleaze ball. He hired the P.I. to find the girl. I've got Harding's address and am going to have a go at him."

"What about the P.I.?"

"Jacob Canoe is his name. He works for Morgan Investigations in Wichita."

Thirty

The chief pushed an intercom button and spoke, "Give me a complete report on a private investigator out of Wichita, Kansas. His name is Jacob Canoe."

He turned back to Enders, "Do you think Harding knows what we know about the girl?"

"I'm sure he does, why else would he pay a lot of money for an out of state investigator?"

"Have you had any contact with the P.I.?"

"Not yet, he's keeping a step ahead of me. He moved out of the hotel that Harding had him in. He's registered in a beachside motel in El Segundo. I went by but he wasn't there."

"Hmm, that's interesting. I wonder why he moved. Do you think that Canoe knows about the girl?"

"Well, Harding is not going to tell him, but who knows what he's found out during his investigation."

"Okay, so what's your next move?"

"I'm going to contact Harding to see what he knows. I've got a lead on his home address. If that doesn't work out I'm going to find this Canoe guy. But, I need to know what my limitations are. We've already got someone, maybe Harding, who doesn't mind a little torture and murder."

There was a knock on the door. "Come in," the chief said.

A woman entered carrying a stack of paper. She set it on the desk.

"We've received a print out of material on Jacob Canoe," she said.

"Thank you Emma," the chief said, taking the manila folder from her. "Close the door behind you, please."

He opened it and began reading the report. He started shaking his head, "Oh damn," he said.

"What's the matter?" Enders asked.

"The report on Canoe, he's ex-special forces. He was recruited by us, but turned it down. Military intelligence has most of his record under wraps. Here's something that sounds ominous. His number of known kills is classified. I'll make a call and see if I can find out more. He sounds like someone you might want to steer clear of, if you can. Here's his picture, take a good look at it. He's in uniform but it doesn't state when the photo was taken. His appearance may have changed."

Enders stared at the picture for a few moments, and then handed the file back to Jackson. "He's not bullet proof, I still need to know what level my priority is."

The chief stood and paced the floor for thirty seconds. He returned to his desk, picked up the report, flipped through the pages, and read more.

"I'm concerned about this Canoe guy, maybe we should bring him into the loop and make a plea to his patriotism. You know, we could convince him that the girl is vital to national security. We might be able to encourage him to give up the girl if he finds her."

"And, what if he doesn't?"

"Do what you have to, but don't leave a trail back to this office. The reason behind this operation is between the two of us for now. Take two agents with you, but they don't need to know the depth of the investigation. If you find the girl don't bring her here, take her to the San Fernando yard."

There was a knock at the door, "Come in," the chief said.

Thirty

The same woman that had brought the report in opened the door. "Agent Enders has a phone call," she said.

"Thank you Emma, go ahead George, take the call. That's all for now, keep me informed of your progress."

Enders went to his office and picked up the phone, "This is Enders."

"Why are you following and asking questions about me?"

"Who is this?"

"You know who this is. I'm the last guy you want to find."

"Okay, Canoe, all I want is the girl. Where is she?"

"I don't know yet, but you're never going to see her."

"Look Canoe, this is bigger than a kidnapping. If you deter me in any way you could be considered as abetting a crime. I can get you in some big trouble."

"Let me make this clear, Enders, I will eventually find the girl, but no one, including you, is going to be able to manipulate or use her for any reason. If you do anything to that girl or harm her in any way, there's no place you can hide. Do not try to follow me again, the last thing you want to do is find me." I hung up.

THIRTY ONE

We cleared out my room, threw all my clothes into the car and left for San Pedro. We opted for the coastal route instead of freeways 405 and 110. We took Grand Avenue east to Sepulveda and headed south. When we crossed Artesia Boulevard in Hermosa Beach, Sepulveda is called the Pacific Coast Highway. The PCH curves back east through Torrance, and into Lomita, where we turned south on Western Avenue. Five or six miles later we were in San Pedro and drove to Tina's house. I waited at the curb while she pulled her Jeep out of the garage. I followed her about a mile to a shopping center that had a twenty four hour grocery. I parked the rental in a slot near the street and climbed into the Jeep with Tina. I still hadn't figured how Enders found the car in Venice but I didn't want to leave it anywhere near Tina's house. When we got back to her place, Tina changed clothes and called the hospital. After a few minutes she hung up.

"My mom's awake and talking. I want to go see her now."

Tina drove to the hospital. When we arrived, I asked. "Do you want me to come in with you?"

Thirty One

"Sure," Tina answered.

A nurse led us to the room. "We called the police and told them that your mother's awake," she said. "They're coming soon to interview her."

The lighting was the usual hospital dim. I could hear beeping noises from other rooms and an intercom voice paging staff to go here or there. Tina's mother looked up when we entered. She had a wrapping on her head. Tina leaned over and kissed her mother on the cheek.

"Is that a policeman?" her mother asked, looking at me.

"No Momma, he's a friend, his name is Jacob."

"Hello, are you the Jacob that was coming to see me?"

"Yes, Missus Flores, I'm sorry they got to you before I did."

"What did they want, Momma?" Tina asked.

"They were asking about the missing baby and then about Annie Gilchrist, and how they could find her. They didn't know her full name, only that her name was Ann or Annie. I didn't know who they were, and at first wouldn't tell them anything, but they started hitting me. When the tall one with the goatee took out a knife, I knew they would kill me unless I told him what they wanted to know. I finally gave them her address. That's when I lost consciousness."

"Do you know why they were looking for her?" Tina asked.

"No, they didn't say."

"Momma, I want you to do me a favor. Don't tell the police about Annie Gilchrist."

"Why not, what should I tell them?"

"Tell them that they tried to rob you or that they were at the wrong house. Tell them anything, just don't mention Annie's name. Jacob is a private investigator and we know why they're looking for Annie. The police won't be able to help but we can."

"Okay Tina, I won't say anything about her. I hope you know what you're doing."

"We do, Momma." Tina saw that her mother's eyes kept closing. "You get some rest, I'll see you tomorrow."

When we got to the parking lot, I dug out the business card given to me by Harding. "Let's go to Harding's office and get some answers."

THIRTY TWO

When Enders and his crew arrived at Harding's house, Enders rang the doorbell. The other two agents were standing to each side of the door, out of sight. When the door opened, Enders stuck a gun in the woman's face.

"Let's go in, don't make a sound."

The three agents went in, closing the door behind them.

"Where is he?" Enders asked.

"In the back," she answered, trembling.

"Let's go, and keep your mouth shut."

She led them down a hall to the rear of the house. Enders kept the gun barrel jammed in her back.

When they entered the room Harding demanded, "Who are you, what do you want?"

"Where's the girl?" Enders asked.

"What girl?"

Enders pointed the gun at the woman and pulled the trigger. She screamed and fell to the floor. He swung the gun back at Harding.

"All right guys, break his thumbs."

The other two agents started for him. "No, please, I'll tell you. She's in Long Beach, don't hurt us."

Enders handed him a note pad and pen, "Write down the address, if it's wrong we'll come back and kill you."

That threat gave Harding hope. *Maybe they're going to let me go if I tell them where she's at.* He wrote the address where Cecil was holding Jamie.

Enders motioned to one of the agents, "Check out the other rooms."

"Is this the correct address?" Enders asked.

"I swear it is, please don't kill me."

When the bullet went through his forehead, Harding's body jerked and then dropped to the floor.

The agent returned, "Hey Enders, there's a woman tied to a chair and blindfolded in the next room over."

"What does she look like?"

He shrugged, "Some older woman."

"You say she's blindfolded and couldn't see you."

"Yeah."

"I wonder who she is and what that's all about?" Enders said, to no one in particular.

He thought about it for ten seconds and then shrugged his shoulders.

"Hmm, well hell, we'll let her live. We've got an address for the girl, that's all we want. Let's get out of here."

THIRTY THREE

We left the hospital with Tina driving and headed north on the harbor freeway. When we reached the 405, Tina took it to Santa Monica Boulevard where we exited. I was navigating when I spotted the building.

"That's it, pull into the underground parking."

Tina drove in and stopped at the ticket dispenser. She pushed a red button, the time stamped stub kicked out and she pulled it from the dispenser. The arm lifted and we drove in. After parking we rode an elevator from the garage up to the lobby and went to the interior elevators.

"It must be on the eighth floor." I said, looking at the address.

We exited the elevator and walked down the hall past a janitor waxing the floor. We found the office number for the law offices of Baxter Harding and saw his name on the door. When I tried the door, I found it was locked. I rapped on the door and got no response.

"There's no one in there," the janitor said.

"No hours are shown on the door. Do you know when they're usually around?" I asked.

"Well," he shut off the waxing buffer, "No one's ever around. It's been vacant for a couple weeks."

"Vacant?" Tina asked.

"Yeah, there's a desk with a phone, but that's all. Everything else was moved out."

"Do you have a key?" I asked, flashing my badge, knowing that no one actually took a hard look at it.

Tina casually put her hands on her hips. The action pulled her jacket back, showing the gun on her hip.

"Sure, officers," the janitor answered, "but there's nothing in there."

"We're detectives, not officers," Tina said, with so much authority that I was almost convinced.

"Uh, yeah, detectives, let me get it unlocked."

He selected a key from a ring hanging on his belt, unlocked and opened the door. We all walked into the office, and as the janitor said, it was empty except for the desk. Tina picked up the phone receiver and put it to her ear.

"It's dead."

The janitor nodded his head, "I told you."

"All right, Tina, let's get out of here."

"Thank you." I said to the janitor. I heard him relocking the door as we walked away.

I looked at Tina when we were in the elevator, "Detectives?"

She smiled, "My childhood dream, I've always wanted to say that."

When we got back to the Jeep, I thought for a few minutes, and then pulled out my note pad and reached into the back seat for the street map.

"I showed an address to Tina, "Do you know where this is?"

Thirty Three

"Yes, the city of Hawthorne is about forty five minutes from here. I can drive there without a map."

"Okay, let's go, we're going to visit someone." I said.

"Who is it we're going to see?"

"He's an ex-employee of Harding. His name's Paul Kotski, AKA Packy."

"He used to work for Harding?"

"Yeah, I convinced him to try a different line of work. He might know how to get to Harding's house."

Tina stopped when we arrived in Hawthorne and consulted the map for the exact street location. We drove block after block past apartment buildings, and finally Tina pulled into a parking lot in front of a two story building.

"Apartment 206 will be upstairs." Tina said.

We went up the exterior stairs to a landing and followed it to number 206. I knocked on the door.

When the door opened we watched Packy step back and put his hands up in a surrender gesture. "I haven't followed you or done anything, Mister Canoe."

"I know, Packy, I'm here to ask for your help, may we step in?"

"Sure, come on in." He stuck his head out the door and looked both ways before closing it. "Sit down," he said.

We both looked around the apartment which was fairly clean but the furniture was ready for the dump. The couch was grubby looking and sweat stained so Tina chose to sit in a wooden chair at the kitchen table. I followed her lead and took a chair next to her.

We watched as Packy carefully eased himself back onto the couch.

"How are your ribs?" I asked.

"Getting better, still taped up, who's the doll?" He nodded toward Tina.

Packy didn't seem to hold a grudge against me for his injuries. He must have figured it was a hazard of the occupation.

"This is Tina. Cecil put her mother in the hospital."

"I swear, I didn't have anything to do with it, I quit working for Harding. I only drove him until he asked me to follow you."

"We know. I want Harding's home address."

"I always picked him up at his office on Santa Monica. I was at his house once or twice but Cecil was driving and it was dark. It's up in the hills above Hollywood. I wouldn't be able to find it again."

"What about Cecil? Where does he live?"

We waited while Packy picked up his cigarettes and shook one out. He lit up and inhaled deeply. He coughed, and winced as he put a hand on his bandaged ribs.

"I heard he lives in a guest house at Harding's place, find Harding and you'll find Cecil."

"Was that your car or his you were driving on Highland?"

"That was one of Harding's cars."

"All right Packy, thanks, are you working?"

"Naw, I've got something lined up in a week or so, as soon as I'm feeling better. It's a nice safe job, parking cars at a fancy restaurant."

I dropped a couple bills on the table. "So long Packy, here's a little cash to hold you over."

His eyes lit up, "Thanks, Mister Canoe."

Thirty Three

When we got to the Jeep, Tina turned to me, "You're a softy, after all."

"I consider him another of Harding's victims, even though he was working for him."

"What was that about the car?"

"It occurred to me that I've got the plate number and know the guy that can trace it to an address."

"Are you talking about Sid?"

"Yep, let's find a phone."

Tina started the Jeep and we pulled out onto the street.

"Where're we going now?" She asked.

"It's been a long time since breakfast, let's get something to eat." I said.

"Good idea," Tina answered. "I'm ready for some food. We're only a few blocks from a great café over on Hawthorne Boulevard. You can use the pay phone there."

Tina had us there in ten minutes and parked in the rear lot. We walked around the building and entered the front door.

"Seat yourselves!" The waitress shouted from behind the counter.

We slid into a tufted booth. I looked around and saw chrome and vinyl, definitely a décor out of the fifties.

I ordered a BLT with onion rings. Tina ordered a tuna sandwich with coleslaw. I spotted the telephone in a hallway leading to the restrooms.

I opened my note pad and pulled out Sid's business card while walking to the phone. I dropped in a quarter and dialed. Sid answered on the first ring.

"Hello Sid, this is Jake. I need a home address for Harding. His office on Santa Monica is a front, nothing in there but an empty desk and a dead phone. I've got the plate number from a car he owns, if that will help."

"That might do, what do you have?"

I read the number. "How long will it take?" I asked.

"Not too long, maybe fifteen minutes at most, where are you?"

"We're at a place called the Hawthorne Grille, getting ready to have a late lunch, or an early dinner."

"Okay, call me when you've finished, I should have something for you by the time you've finish eating."

I returned to the booth just as the waitress brought our food. I plopped down across from Tina.

"What did he say?" She asked.

"I'm going to call back after we're done eating, he may have an address for Harding by then."

"What do you think the C.I.A. agent wants?"

"I'm not sure, but it must have something to do with the girl, Jamie."

"Why would they want her?"

"This is going to sound crazy, but they all seem to think she has some form of ESP. Whatever they want, you know it's not going to be good for Jamie."

"Is that what Jamie meant, in the van, when she said that they thought she could read minds."

"Yeah, and a lot of others seem to think the same thing."

"What others?"

"Some of the nurses from the hospital believed it."

"What do you think?"

Thirty Three

"I don't know, but when I was a kid, my best friend was an old Apache Indian who claimed to have visions about the future. Everything he predicted for me came true."

"What happened to him?"

"He died a few years ago, he was very old."

"What did he predict for you?"

"It's something I don't want to talk about now, maybe someday I'll tell you."

"I'm sorry, Jake, I didn't mean to pry."

"That's all right, I'm just pointing out that I'm not discounting claims that Jamie may have some kind of psychic ability. I know my old friend Sam did have something like that, but I can't explain it."

"What do you think Jamie was talking about in the van? The dream with an old Indian was kind of weird."

"I don't know, Tina."

"She seemed to think you were in the dream too."

"It doesn't make any sense, we had never met before. She described my old friend Sam to a tee. I can't explain it, let's finish eating and get out of here."

"Okay Jake, I'm done, let's go."

I handed Tina a twenty. "You pay the check. I'll call Sid and see if he's come up with an address for Harding from the car plate."

A minute later, I had Sid on the phone. "What'd you find out?"

"This should be his home address." Sid said, reading it to me.

I wrote down the residence address that he gave me.

"He also owns some commercial warehouses around the city, do you want those too?"

"No, not now, I'm going to his house first."

Tina was waiting for me at the door. We went to the Jeep with Tina getting behind the wheel. I opened the map book to locate Harding's address.

"It's off a street called Coldwater Canyon," I said. "It looks like there are a lot of curvy streets up in those hills. We'll definitely need the map."

"I know the general area," Tina said, "It's near Beverly Hills and Hollywood. When we're on Coldwater you can direct us in. It's getting late, so it'll probably be getting dark by the time we get there."

"Dark could be good, let's go."

An hour later, we parked at the curb in front of a large two story house. A low un-gated stone wall ran along the property front. There were two auto entrances with a circular paved driveway. The sun had dropped behind the mountains to the west, which made it difficult to see the house features. All the lots were large so the neighboring houses were some distance away. The smell of fresh cut grass hung in the air. The only noise was a barking dog, seemingly coming from behind a house across the street. The dog was probably alerted by the unfamiliar sound of the Jeep.

Tina unsnapped a flashlight from a bracket on the steering column and we climbed out of the Jeep.

We crept up the driveway, staying to one side under a row of eucalyptus trees. The formidable looking front door was at least eight feet tall with two dim porch lights, one on each side. The lower floor appeared to be dark, but a window on the upper floor was backlit with light.

"Let's go around to the back and see if we can find a way in." I said.

Thirty Three

Now that we were closer, I could see the house was Spanish style architecture with corbels and scuppers along the roofline. We followed a paved path around one side to the rear of the house and then through a wooden gate into the courtyard.

The pool was surrounded by several patio tables with chairs. Each table had an umbrella over it. There were half a dozen chaise lounge's scattered around. Once inside the gate we took a brick walk to the deck between the pool and house. The only sound was the humming of the pool pump motor. We could see a muted glow from lighting in the rear room. The back wall had large windows with a sliding door. I edged my way along the wall and peered around into the house. I saw that there was no one in the room. I tested the door, but it was locked and would not move.

"Let's check the guesthouse." I whispered. "We'll see if his man, Cecil, is here."

"I hope so," Tina said, "I'm not done with him yet."

We followed the walkway around to the other side of the house and spotted a small cottage. A window was illuminated by an inside light.

"Wait here," I said, as I sidled to the window for a look inside.

There was no one in sight, and I could see a TV set that was off. I tried the door knob and found it was unlocked. I slowly opened the door and stepped in to make sure no one was there. It was a one room place with a double bed and small kitchenette. The bathroom door was wide open and I could see no one was in there. Convinced that Cecil was gone, I went out and closed the door behind me.

"Jake," I heard Tina whisper.

I turned and saw her pointing at a cellar door toward the other end of the house. We went to the door and saw that it had a hasp with padlock.

It was a typical old basement entrance with a concrete frame around the steps and a wooden door installed at an angle to prevent rain water from getting in. The wood looked old and weather beat. I stuck my fingers under the edge of the door and started pulling up.

The rusty screws holding the hasp pulled half way out of the rotten wood. I gave it a good yank, the screws pulled loose and the hasp and lock were hanging free.

We paused for thirty seconds and listened for any sound or reaction that we had been heard. All was quiet so I laid the door back, wide open.

Tina handed the flashlight to me and I led the way down the steps into the musty smelling cellar.

"Yuk," I heard Tina say. She was brushing webs from her face and clothes as she followed me.

I swung the light around at the many boxes, filing cabinets, discarded furniture and other household items. We made our way through the debris to a stairway going up to the main floor.

"Let's hope the door going into the house is unlocked." I said.

I paused at the top of the stairs, slowly turned the knob and opened the door about six inches. I could see a hallway, partially lit by light from another room. I opened the door further and stepped into the hall with Tina on my heels.

I quietly closed the door behind us and we started up the hallway. We stopped when we heard a low moan. We moved up the hall to an open door where the light was coming from. Tina drew her gun and nodded at me. We both stepped into the room.

Harding was on the floor with blood pooled around his head. His coat and tie were draped over a chair back. His sleeves were rolled up to

Thirty Three

his elbows. A woman was sitting on the floor with her back against a wall. The front of her blouse was covered with blood. Tina knelt down and put her fingers on the woman's throat feeling for a pulse. The woman moaned at the touch and opened her eyes.

"Who did this to you?" Tina asked.

"I don't know who he was."

"What did he look like?"

"He was bald, wearing a suit."

Tina and I looked at each other.

"Are you Missus Harding, formerly Doctor Janet Gresso?" I asked.

"Yes," the woman weakly answered.

Tina held her by the shoulders, "Tell us where Jamie is."

The woman blinked her eyes and said, "Signal Hill."

"Signal Hill, what's that?" I asked, looking at Tina.

"It's at the north end of Long Beach, off the 405 freeway. I know how to get there," Tina answered.

"What's the address," I asked the woman.

She opened her mouth trying to speak when suddenly her eyes closed and her head slumped down.

Tina felt for a pulse again, then looked at me, and shook her head, "She's dead."

"Did you hear her say it was a bald man?" Tina asked.

"I think we know who that is."

"Yes we do, it appears that our C.I.A. agent is a murderer."

"Sid said that Harding owned several warehouses, maybe one of them is at Signal Hill," I said.

We heard another loud moan. We looked at each other.

Tina pulled her gun and edged over to the next room. She turned the doorknob and swung the door open. The room was dark, Tina yelled, "Who's there?"

We heard a feeble voice cry, "Help me."

Tina found the light switch and flipped it on. We both stepped into the room.

A nude blindfolded woman was tied to a chair in the center of the room. A hand cranked generator with leads was on a table along with a pile of clothes. Tina holstered her gun, removed the blindfold and began untying the ropes.

"Are you Jamie's mother?" Tina asked.

"Yes, do you know where she is?"

"Maybe, but not for sure, we are going to find her," I said.

"Something happened in the next room," she said, "I heard loud voices and gunshots. A few minutes later I heard someone open the door like they were looking in here but they closed it without saying anything. Then I heard footsteps tromping down the hall and a door slammed. Then it was quiet until you got here."

When I picked up the phone, Jamie's mother said. "Please don't call the police or an ambulance, I don't want them involved."

I think I know why. I thought. *There's no statute of limitation on kidnapping.*

"I'm calling someone else, not the police," I said.

That seemed to placate her.

I dialed Sid's number, after ten rings I hung up.

"Damn, Sid's not answering, we'll have to call in the morning. I should have got the warehouse addresses when I had him on the phone."

Thirty Three

"We've got to help this woman." Tina said. "I'll get her dressed and we'll take her to a hospital."

"No, take me home, I don't need a hospital." The woman said.

"Are you sure?" I asked.

"I'm fine, just worn out, I only need some rest."

"Your home may not be safe for now. We'll take you to my house. You'll be safe there until we find Jamie." Tina told her.

"Who are you two?"

"I'll explain later, for now, just know that we're going to find Jamie." Tina answered.

"I'll wait for you two in the Jeep," I said.

I left the room and headed for the front door.

Thirty minutes later we were on the freeway heading to San Pedro. It was night time, the freeway traffic was not as congested as during the day, and everyone was driving faster than us. One driver was recklessly swapping lanes, but wasn't making better time than we were.

As soon as we arrived at Tina's place she called the hospital to check on her mother. After a few minutes of conversation she hung up and turned to me.

"She's raising a fuss about being released from the hospital, let's go get her."

"Will you be okay if we leave for a while?" Tina asked Jamie's mother.

"I'll be fine, thank you for getting me out of there."

On the way to the hospital, Tina said, "I know my mother will want to go to her house. Do you think she'll be okay there?"

"Yeah, they won't be coming back to her place. Harding's men got all the information from your mother that they wanted."

Tina signed the paper work to check her mother out of the hospital. We went to the parking lot and got into Tina's Jeep.

"Do you want to go home with me, Mom?" Tina asked.

"No, I'm ready to sleep in my own bed."

"Are you sure, are you going to be okay?"

"I'll be fine, Tina, I don't need a babysitter."

"All right, Mom." Tina said, smiling at me with that "I told you so" look.

It took about thirty minutes to get Tina's mother to her house. Tina went in with her and was back in five minutes, so we headed to Tina's house. There was nothing more we could do until I contacted Sid in the morning.

THIRTY FOUR

"This is it," Enders said, pointing at the building. The driver parked on a side street, "How shall we do it?" He asked.

"Too much traffic out front, we'll go in the back door." Enders answered.

They exited the car. One of the agents popped the trunk and took out a sledge hammer. They headed for the back door. Enders and the other agent pulled their guns and stepped to the side. The agent with the hammer spread his legs in a stance, lined up the target spot on the door, pulled back the hammer and swung. The lock assembly shattered and the door flew open.

All three ran in the door with guns drawn.

"Don't shoot, I'm not armed," Cecil yelled, raising his hands.

Enders immediately shot him. "Check out the rest of the place," he shouted, smiling at the girl taped to the chair.

One of the agents disappeared around a corner. Twenty seconds later they heard two gunshots. He returned putting his gun back into his holster. "Guy was sitting on the crapper, unarmed."

"Yeah, this one wasn't packing either. Now I feel bad about shooting him."

They all laughed at his humor.

"Hi there sweetie, what's your name?"

"I'm Jamie, are you here to help me?"

"We sure are, Jamie. Why were they holding you?"

"They have some crazy idea that I can read minds, they're holding my mother somewhere to make me do what they want."

"Holding your mother?" Enders asked.

"Yes, I don't know where she is."

"Get her loose." Enders told one of the agents.

He pulled the other man to the side and whispered to him.

"Listen, Parker, the woman tied up at Harding's house must be her mother. We screwed up leaving her there, but at least we didn't kill her. We'll drive to the office so you can get another car and go grab the mother. I want you to stash her somewhere. We'll take the girl to the yard, and keep them separated. Harding's basic idea was good. They just didn't have the resources or brains to pull it off."

They headed back to the office with Enders and Jamie in the back seat, the other two in front.

"Who are you? I know you're not the police. Police wouldn't just shoot those guys and leave them."

"Smart girl, we're with the government." Enders showed her his badge.

"Where are we going? Do you know where my mother is?" Jamie asked.

Thirty Four

"We're looking for her. We'll take you to a safe place until we find her."

"Can you take me home?"

"There's no one there to watch you, you'll be okay with us."

"I can take care of myself. I don't need to be watched."

"I'm sure you don't, Jamie, but please humor me for now." He reached over and put his hand on hers.

She pulled her hand from his grasp, "Don't do that," she said, moving over in the seat. She turned and stared out the window.

Enders shrugged when the driver turned, looked at him and grinned.

When they reached the office, the driver pulled to the curb. Enders and the front passenger both got out.

Enders turned to the driver, "I'm going to stay here at the office for now but I'll see you later at the yard. Agent Parker is going to Harding's house to take care of that matter we talked about. Wait here, I'll send someone out to accompany you to take Jamie to the yard."

Enders started for the building, looking back, he told Parker, "Call me here when you're finished at Harding's."

A few minutes later, a woman came out and got into the rear seat with Jamie.

"Hi Jamie, my name's Carol, I'm going to stay with you for a while." Another man got into the front passenger seat.

"Okay, let's go to the yard," she said to the driver.

"What's the yard?" Jamie asked.

"It's a nice place to stay until we find your mother."

"When are we going to start looking for my mother?"

"We've got people looking now. We want you to be safe."

"I'm running out of patience, why don't we go to the police?"

"That's no good Jamie. We're better equipped than the police."

"What about Jacob Canoe, do you know where he is?"

"Who's he? I've never heard of him." Carol answered.

I'd feel safer with him and Tina, Jamie thought, *they found me once and I'll bet they can find my mother.*

"He'll find me soon and will help me find my mother."

An hour later they were in San Fernando. Jamie was puzzled as they drove down a street lined with commercial properties. There were no houses, only warehouses, auto wrecking yards and weed covered storage yards.

"What's this, where are we going?" Jamie asked. "I thought we were going to a nice place."

"It's better than being taped to a chair," the driver said.

The driver pulled into a short driveway and stopped. He exited the car and unlocked the padlock on a chain link fence. He opened the gate, got back into the car, drove through the gate, got out and relocked it. They proceeded between two rows of cement block buildings, stopping at the last one.

"What is this place?" Jamie asked, looking at Carol.

It was cement block construction like the others and had large rollup and pedestrian doors. There was no sign, only a large obscure building.

"It's nicer inside." Carol said.

Jamie was surprised to see a fully furnished office with two desks, filing cabinets, several chairs and a couch. There were four TV screens

Thirty Four

on a shelf with each showing different outside areas. Jamie could see the gate they had come through on one of the screens. One camera was showing an outside view of the front door.

A man at one of the desks was speaking on a phone. He looked up and smiled as they walked through to another door. He reached under the desk and there was an audible buzz. Carol opened the door.

They stepped into a posh living room with wall to wall carpeting. It appeared to be professionally decorated with nice furniture, tables and lamps. The concrete walls were painted and pictures were hung. There was a television standing along a wall. At the end of the room was a full kitchen with stove, refrigerator and all the accoutrements of a modest home. Jamie could see a hallway with doors. She decided that there must be at least one bathroom and the other doors may be for bedrooms. *What an odd place,* she thought.

"I think you'll be comfortable here." Carol said.

"Where can I sleep? I've hardly slept for two days." Jamie said.

"First room on the left, down that hall," Carol said, pointing.

"I'm tired, I'm going to take a nap," Jamie said.

"Okay Jamie, I'll wake you when agent Enders arrives. He'll want to interview you and give you some tests."

"What do you mean? Interview and tests? I'm not doing any tests and I don't need to be interviewed."

"I'll let agent Enders explain that to you when he gets here."

"The only thing I want explained is, when are you going to find my mother?"

"I'm sure they're working on it right now."

"They better be!" Jamie shouted as she stormed into her assigned room and slammed the door.

She lay staring at the ceiling. *I'm getting fed up with all these people.* She closed her eyes and was asleep in seconds. The Indian was smiling at her. He reached out and put a hand on each side of her head. She heard his voice, "Do not worry, he is coming for you."

THIRTY FIVE

The next morning I called Sid at 8 A.M. He answered on the first ring. "Ajax Detective Agency, Sid speaking."

"Hi, Sid, this is Jake Canoe. Is one of Harding's warehouses in Long Beach?"

"Yes, he has one on Cherry Avenue at Signal Hill. Grab your pen and I'll give you the address."

"Okay, go ahead." I wrote down the address.

"Thanks Sid, I'll be in touch," we both hung up.

"We've got an address, Tina. Let's get on the road for Long beach."

"We're going to leave you again." Tina told Jamie's mother. "We've got a lead on where Jamie may be. Make yourself at home."

Thirty minutes later we exited the 405 freeway onto Cherry Boulevard. We cruised the street until Tina said, "There it is, that building on the corner."

She drove past the warehouse and parked curbside near the intersection.

We turned in our seats and looked back at the large old wooden building. It had a roofed porch on the front. It appeared to have been built around the turn of the century. On the side street was located a loading dock with a large roll up door. The door was closed and all the side windows were high on the walls. The front windows were large with closed venetian blinds. The place seemed deserted except for one car parked next to the loading dock. The street traffic was light.

"What now?" Tina asked.

"We have to figure a way to get inside."

"There's a skylight on the roof," Tina said. "Maybe you can get up there and take a look inside."

"Good idea, there's probably an outside maintenance ladder. You wait here while I scout around the building."

The warehouse was located high on a hill and I could see industrial buildings and vacant lots across the valley below me. There were oil derricks, large holding tanks and hundreds of oil pumps going up and down sucking that valuable black nectar out of the ground.

Tina watched as Jake walked to and around the corner. Then he came into sight briefly at the rear corner of the warehouse. Tina waited nervously, watching for any sign that he might need help. A few minutes later she saw movement on the roof and saw it was Jake. He had somehow found a way to the top of the building.

I climbed up a maintenance ladder affixed to the rear outside wall, then crept across the roof to an elevated skylight where I knelt down. I cupped my hands on the sides of my eyes to shield the sunlight as I looked in. I could see a man sprawled on the floor with a dark pool of blood around his head. I looked down to the street and could see Tina watching from the car so I motioned her over and then headed back to the ladder. Tina was waiting for me by the time I was down to the ground.

"What's up?" she asked.

"There's a man's body on the floor, I couldn't see anyone else. Let's see if we can get in."

We went up wood steps to a rear door. I pushed on the door and it hinged open. The inside jamb was splintered and broken.

"That was easy," Tina said.

"Someone beat us here." I said.

I walked to the corpse, leaned down and peered at the face. There was a bullet hole in the forehead. "Well, so much for Cecil." I said.

"I'll check out the rest of the place," Tina said.

She pulled her pistol and began searching the building. It was vacant except for a front counter, a lot of empty shelving and filing cabinets. An empty chair sat in the middle of the floor with cut duct tape lying next to it. She went first to a front office and looked it over. It was empty except for an old oak desk. The bathroom door was partially open. Tina kicked it open all the way with her gun pointing in, and saw a man slumped on the toilet with his pants around his ankles.

"We've got another body in the restroom," she yelled, "Gunshot wounds to the head and chest."

She came back in, knelt and felt the side of Cecil's face.

"It must have been several hours, he's cold and the blood's dry."

"Well, Jamie's not here. I guess we know who has her now." I said.

"Are you thinking that it's our bald CIA agent?"

"Yeah, he must really want her. The bodies are starting to pile up."

I pulled out the card he left with the motel manager.

"His name is George Enders. I warned him to leave Jamie alone. She must have been taped to this chair. He's starting to piss me off."

"Do you think he's sanctioned to go around killing people to get Jamie?"

"Maybe, or he might be working on his own."

"I don't understand. Why would the CIA be interested in her?"

"I'm not sure, maybe it's about the ESP business, but we've got to find her."

"What do we do next?" Tina asked.

"We'll start at the address on his card."

I showed it to Tina, "This must be the CIA office he works out of, any idea where it is?"

"Yes, that's downtown Los Angeles."

"All right, let's head there."

We left through the back door and crossed the street to the Jeep.

After fighting traffic into town, we located the address on Hill Street. We pulled into a pay to park lot directly across the street from the office building. We paid the attendant and received a receipt. Tina found a parking space on the outside row next to the sidewalk.

We were staring directly across the street at the CIA building. It was a modern three story sandwiched between older buildings. Half the lot was designated for parking and was surrounded by a tall chain link fence. A red and white striped crossing arm was in the lowered position blocking access to the lot. We could see a lone man in the guard shack. The building had no name, only the address.

"Okay, Detective, what do we do now?" Tina asked.

Thirty Five

I thought for a minute, and then said, "I'll be right back."

Tina waited while I walked to a pay phone booth. I stepped in and closed the folding door. I pulled out the business card that Enders had left at the motel and dialed the number. Twenty seconds later, I exited the booth, returned to the jeep and slid into the passenger seat.

"Well, now let's see what happens." I said.

The receptionist in the CIA building answered the phone and paged Enders.

"Agent Enders, someone called and said you have a flat tire."

"Who called?" He asked.

"I don't know, someone in the downstairs office, I guess."

Exasperated, he stood from his desk, "Great, that's all I need."

He took the elevator down to the main floor and exited to the parking lot. He walked around his car, checking the tires.

I don't have a flat, he thought, *the left rear looks a little low, but not flat. Maybe that's what they saw.*

Three minutes later we watched the bald man with sun glasses come rushing out of a side door into the parking lot. We saw him go to a black four door sedan and walk around it. He stared at the car for a few moments and then shook his head. He finally returned to the building.

"What did you do?" Tina asked.

"I called the number on his card. I told them to tell Enders that he has a flat tire and hung up."

"I get it, so now we know he's in there and which car is his." Tina said.

"Yeah, that was the plan, now we'll have to sit back and wait. When he leaves, we'll follow him. If we're lucky he'll lead us to Jamie."

"What if they have her in there?"

"Maybe they do, but it may be tough to get past their security. There are six cars in the parking lot, so at least that many people are in the building. There may be others coming and going. Enders must know where she is, we'll start by asking him."

"So, how long are we prepared to wait for him?"

"It's after four now, he'll probably be leaving by five, we'll see what happens."

Enders went back into the building and looked around the first floor office. "Who said I have a flat tire?" The three people in the office shrugged, shook their heads and went back to work.

Enders took the elevator back up to his floor and stopped at the receptionist desk.

"My tires are okay, about time I had some luck."

The receptionist said, "I hope it's not about to change, you've got a call from agent Parker, he says it's urgent."

Enders picked up an extension, "What's up, Parker?"

"She's gone."

"What?"

"Her mother's not here. I did a full search of the house, she's long gone."

Thirty Five

"Damn, she must have gotten loose," he lowered his voice, "Are the bodies still there?"

"Yep, just like we left them."

"All right, let's think this through. She didn't see us, and she's not going to go to the cops if she kidnapped the baby. The girl doesn't know her mother is free so we still have that leverage."

"What do you want me to do now?"

"Go to the yard, we've got agents with the kid. I'm going to leave for there soon."

Enders hung up and dialed Carol at the yard, "How's she doing?"

"She's not happy."

"As soon as I get there, we'll start doing some tests, I'm anxious to see what she's capable of."

"It may not be as easy as you think. What if she doesn't cooperate?"

"We'll promise to reunite her with her mother as soon as she does what we want."

"I don't know how long that'll work, she seems pretty stubborn."

"If I have to, I'm prepared to use some extreme measures."

"What do you mean by that?"

"We'll start with sodium pentothal."

"I've read reports that it doesn't work that well and the information result is unreliable. I also think it's illegal except for medical purposes."

"What do you suggest, Carol, pulling out her fingernails?"

"I hope you're kidding, I don't think torture is going to be necessary."

"I've gone too far to back down now. I've spent half my career trying to find someone with paranormal abilities. This is as close as I've been."

"Oh, by the way, who is Jacob Canoe?" Asked Carol.

The line went silent. "Hello, Enders, you still there?" she asked.

His voice was strained when he finally answered.

"Yes I'm here, where did you hear that name?"

"From Jamie, he's someone she knows, says he'll find her and her mother."

"I'm getting out of here in a few minutes, Carol. I'll see you in about an hour."

He hung up as the secretary came to his door.

"Chief Jackson wants to see you in his office," she said.

Enders knocked, "Come in," he heard the chief say.

When he went in, a man he didn't know was standing in front of Jackson's desk.

"You wanted to see me, Mister Jackson?" he asked, puzzled at who the man was.

"Agent Enders, this is Doctor Hermann."

"Hello, Agent Enders," the doctor answered, with a heavy German accent.

Enders stuck his hand out, *who's this old Nazi bastard,* he wondered.

"Doctor Hermann is going to accompany you to the yard to do tests and experiments with the girl."

Enders bristled at that, "Wait a minute, this is my case. I should be able to see it through."

"And you will, Agent Enders, but doctor Hermann has experience in these matters so you are going to assist and observe."

"I really don't need any help, Mister Jackson."

"It's my decision, Enders, I expect you to give the doctor your fullest cooperation. If not I'll have to take you off the case. You'll get full credit for finding her."

Enders answered reluctantly, "Well, okay Chief, no problem. I'll let him do the tests, as you wish."

Thirty Five

Enders watched as the doctor visibly puffed up his chest and jutted his jaw out.

He's obviously pleased with himself, Enders thought. He was sure the doctor was going to click his heels together.

"Okay Doctor, let's go, I'll drive."

They rode the elevator down to the bottom floor and walked out to the parking lot without any conversation. They went to the car, where Enders got in behind the wheel.

Enders started driving to the yard with the doctor sitting quietly in the passenger seat.

He was concerned at what Carol had told him, about the girl saying that Canoe would come for her. *How does she know Canoe?* He wondered. *When could they have met and where is he now? How did Harding get hold of Jamie if Canoe had already found her?*

He suddenly felt frightened and a shudder went through him. He shook it off. *Stop it, he can't find me,* he thought. *He's only a private eye and I'm an armed CIA agent. I should never have left my card with that motel clerk, now he knows my name and our office address. He could…, uh oh,* he thought, *the call about the tire might have been him.* He quickly checked his rear view mirror. The street behind him was packed with traffic. *Could he be back there tailing me?*

"Are you all right, Agent Enders? You seem agitated." The doctor said with a small smile.

"I'm fine Doc, don't worry about me."

THIRTY SIX

Tina started the Jeep when we saw Enders go to his car. "I wonder who that is with him," she said, as they watched a man get into the car with Enders.

"Another CIA spook we'll have to deal with." I answered.

We watched Enders pull onto the street, turn right and head north. Tina drove forward, bumped over the cement tire stop, crossed over the sidewalk and dropped off the curb to follow them.

We were several vehicles behind Enders. "We'll be okay," Tina said, "Unless we get caught by a red light. Should I try to get closer?"

"If we get too close, he might spot us, stay three cars back, about like we are now."

By the time we got to the north end of the valley the traffic had thinned considerably. We were about a block behind Enders with only one vehicle between us. When Enders stopped for a light, Tina would slow, or glide over to the curb, wait for him to proceed, and then pull

Thirty Six

out to follow. When Tina saw Enders signal to turn left, she sped up so as to not lose him.

When we caught up, Enders was parked in a driveway, already out of his car and standing at a gate. The drive ran between two rows of buildings.

"Drive on by, make a U-turn at the next corner, come back and park just short of the drive." I told her, ducking down, so Enders wouldn't see me.

We parked near the gate and looked down the driveway. We could see Ender's car and two others parked at the last building, on the right. Enders and the other man were nowhere in sight.

"They must have gone inside the last building," I said.

"What do you think, could Jamie be in there?" Tina asked.

"Maybe, we'll wait a few minutes and see what happens."

"Check out the fence, Jacob, that's a ten footer with razor wire on top, and it looks like it goes all the way around the lot."

"Yeah, the front gate seems to be the only way in." I answered.

Inside, the agent monitoring the security TV screens had announced, "Enders is at the gate, unknown passenger with him."

After Enders parked, he and Hermann went into the building, where Carol met them.

"Where is she?" Enders asked.

"She's taking a nap in one of the rooms."

"Who's this?" Carol asked, nodding toward the doctor.

"Carol, meet doctor Hermann, Jackson says he's to do all of the testing."

She shot a quick glance at Enders, sensing his displeasure.

"Hello Doctor," Carol said, extending her hand.

The doctor nodded at her, and ignored her hand, without answering. Carol shrugged, looking at Enders.

"Take the doctor back to the interview room. I'll be there in a few minutes with the girl," Enders said.

"Do you have any tools in the Jeep?" I asked Tina. I was beginning to get antsy about what was going on in the warehouse.

"There's a box of stuff back there, what do you want?"

"I'm not sure, but I'll know it when I see it."

I went around to the rear of the Jeep and found the tool box. The first thing I saw when I opened the box, was a paint spattered claw hammer. I set it aside and dug into the other tools to see what I could come up with. The rest was only screwdrivers, pliers, tape measure and a couple of putty knives. I opted for the hammer and closed up the tool box. I walked around and showed Tina the hammer.

"This should do," I said, "I'll be right back."

Tina watched Jake go to the gate, lift the hammer and swing it at the padlock. She saw pieces of the broken lock fall to the ground. Then he unhooked the remains of the lock from the hasp and tossed it aside. He returned to the Jeep and replaced the hammer into the toolbox.

"Wait here, I'm going to see if Jamie is in there." I said.

"Maybe I should go with you. We don't know how many people are in there."

"No, stay here, if I'm not back in twenty minutes, come in, but be careful."

"Here, take my gun," Tina said, unclipping the holster, and handing it to me.

I hesitated a few seconds, and then took the weapon.

"Twenty minutes," I repeated.

I clipped the holster on my belt in the small of my back, and pulled out my shirt to cover it.

I heard and saw no one as I approached the door. When I got near, I saw it was a heavy steel security door.

"Agent Enders," a man watching the monitors inside, had shouted, when he first spotted Jake. "Unknown man coming through the gate, he's on foot, walking toward us."

Enders stared at the monitor, "I've only seen his picture, but that looks like Canoe, the private eye. He must have followed me here."

"What should we do?"

"Unlock the door so he can walk right in." Enders said.

I tried the door knob and was surprised when it easily turned. I pushed the door open and saw a large young man sitting at a desk. He smiled at me.

"Hello, Mister Canoe, come in."

When I stepped in I heard a rustle behind the door. Before I could react something jabbed me in the back. I felt a painful electric shock and fell to the floor with my limbs shaking. I tried to stand but had no strength and felt powerless. Then I was being dragged by the arms to another room where they dropped me in a chair.

Tina kept nervously checking her watch. *I can't believe only five minutes have passed,* she thought. Another five minutes passed, *only ten minutes, it seems he's been gone an eternity.* She was fidgeting and trying to see up the driveway when she spotted something on the first building in the fenced lot. *What's that?* She wondered. There was an object mounted at the edge of the roof line. She opened the glove box, pulled out her binoculars and focused on it. Her breath caught when she saw it was a camera pointed at the gate.

Oh no, they must have seen him coming. How did we miss that?

She sat for a minute, and then decided, *I can't wait any longer.* She got out of the Jeep and walked to the fence, away from the gate, staying out of the view of the camera.

How am I going to get in there without being seen? She wondered. *If I go in through the gate, they'll see me coming.* She could see that the high fence completely encompassed the yard. Then she noticed that the lot next door had a large building next to the fence. It was slightly taller and adjacent to the one that Jake was in.

She walked back down the road and saw that the other yard was full of heavy construction equipment, with only that one building in the rear. The front chain link fence around this yard was shorter, about six feet tall and no razor wire. The yard next door appeared deserted for now and the gate was padlocked. Tina looked up and down the street and assured herself that no one could see her. She grasped the top horizontal fence rail, lifted herself up and vaulted over the fence, landing on her feet on the other side.

She looked around again, saw nothing and heard no sounds of alarm, so she headed toward the building at the rear of the storage lot.

She was wending her way through the yard full of machinery when she heard a low growl behind her. The hair on the back of her neck stood up and her heart started beating faster as the adrenalin kicked in.

Damn, a dog, she thought, *I should have known there might be one.*

She slowly turned her head and saw an Alsatian staring at her inquisitively, with ears at full attention. She was relieved when she saw it wasn't a Doberman or Pit Bull.

She had worked with this breed as a guard in the Marine Corps. Their size was intimidating but unless they were actually trained as an attack or guard dog, they were usually people friendly.

"Come here, puppy," she cooed, patting her leg.

The dog seemed to relax and wagged his tail a bit, "Come on, come here," she said gently. The dog approached her tentatively, sniffed her out stretched hand and licked it. *Whew, he loves me,* she thought with relief.

When she began petting him, the dog jumped around excitably, wagging his tail furiously. She started for the back of the lot to the tall building, with the dog on her heels. The dog was occasionally rubbing it's snout on her leg for more attention.

She saw an air conditioning unit on the roof. *There must be a way to get up there.*

She walked around the building until she found a ladder attached to the rear wall. When she started climbing the steps, the dog looked up at her, whined and danced around in a circle. She paused long enough to pet the dog again and then went on up the ladder. When she reached the top and stepped onto the roof, she heard the dog make a final yelp.

THIRTY SEVEN

I was stunned but not unconscious, "What was that?" I asked, blinking my eyes.

I could see a figure in front of me holding a flashlight looking object.

"It's a cattle prod. You'd be amazed how effective it is on humans."

I recognized the person as Enders.

"You bastards are sick. Tell you what, Enders, let me take Jamie out of here and I won't kill you."

"You're in no position to be making threats, Canoe."

"How do you know I'm working alone? If I found you someone else can."

"Right now, we're only concerned with you."

"You've made too many mistakes, Enders. A lot of people can connect you to me."

Jake reached behind his back and realized the gun was gone.

"Are you looking for this?"

Enders was holding the pistol, smiling.

"After a little ballistic manipulation, something tells me that an investigation is going to find this gun will match a few bodies I've left around."

"You'll never get away with it, Enders."

"You'd be surprised at what I can get away with, Canoe. I want a few answers, now. We'll start with you telling me if you know where the kid's mother is."

"I'm not going to tell you anything, Enders."

Enders shoved the prod on my chest again. I let out a gasp and fell off the chair to the floor. When my body relaxed a few seconds later, I shook my head to clear my thinking. My heart was pounding, my breath ragged and I was dripping with sweat. They lifted me back onto the chair.

Through the haze, I heard Enders speaking, "Okay, let's go see the girl. We'll continue this later."

"What about Canoe? Should I stay here with him?" the other man asked.

"He's in no condition to go anywhere."

The two men left me alone in the room. I tried to stand, but my head was reeling and I fell back into the chair.

Tina walked to the roof edge to gauge how far it was to the other building. *Looks like it's about seven feet,* she thought. She returned to the center of the roof, turned around, and ran for the edge, leaping as far as her momentum would take her. She cleared the space by a foot and rolled when she landed on the other building. *I hope they didn't hear me hit the roof,* she thought.

Thirty Seven

She crept lightly along the edge of the roof and spotted a ladder mounted to the end wall. Continuing to the front of the building, she looked down, and saw a camera aimed at the front door. The camera was mounted about one foot below the roofline. She stretched out on the roof, reached her arm down, grabbed the cable going to the camera and yanked it free. She hustled back to the ladder, climbed down to the ground and raced around to the front door.

Jamie woke when she felt a hand on her shoulder. She looked up and saw Carol leaning over her. It took a few seconds to realize where she was.

"Hi Jamie, did you have a good nap?"

"I guess, but I'll sleep better when I get out of here."

"I'm sure that won't be long, meantime they're ready to see you."

Jamie sat up with an angry look on her face.

"Whatta you mean, they? How many people want to see me?"

"Only two, Agent Enders and Doctor Hermann."

"Why a doctor, I'm not sick, I don't need to see a doctor."

"He wants to do a few tests."

"No way, I told you, I don't want anyone doing tests on me."

"The sooner we get done, the quicker you'll be able to leave."

"Okay, I'll go with you to see what they want, but I'm telling you, I'll leave anytime I want. I'm only staying because I don't know where my mother is."

Carol led her down a hall to a room in the rear. Jamie recognized Enders and the driver of the car that drove them here. An older man, that she presumed was the doctor, was arranging some items on a table.

The driver, sporting the same crew cut and demeanor as Enders was leaning against a wall. Carol went to a couch and sat down.

"Please sit in this comfortable chair, Jamie," said the older man, with an engaging smile.

"Who are you?" Jamie asked.

"I'm Doctor Hermann, I've been told that you are a remarkable young woman. I'd like to find out how remarkable."

"I don't know what you're talking about, doctor." Jamie answered.

The doctor smiled and picked up a syringe from the table and pulled the plunger out. Then Jamie watched the doctor shove the needle into a vial.

"What's that for?"

"This will relax you."

"I don't want to relax, and you're not going to stick me with that."

Enders spoke, "Now Jamie, if you want to see your mother again, you will cooperate."

"I don't threaten easy, Mister Enders." Jamie said.

Jamie watched the doctor point the hypo needle up, and flick the syringe with his middle finger to clear the bubbles. When he slightly depressed the plunger, a fine mist sprayed out. She noticed his hand was trembling and his face was flushed.

"May I ask you something, Doctor?" She asked.

"Certainly you may, my dear."

"You seem nervous, Doc, is this your first time doing this?"

The doctor approached her with the syringe without answering.

"Hold her arm," Enders told the driver.

THIRTY EIGHT

Tina was in front of the door, waiting for someone to open it to check the camera.

I'll give it a minute, if no one comes out, I'll have to hammer on the door and see if I can get some attention.

Then she heard a voice inside yell, "Hey, the door camera quit working, I'm going out to see what's wrong with it."

She moved to one side and flattened her back against the outside wall. When the door opened, a big muscular man stuck his head out and looked up at the camera.

She quietly said, "I'm here."

When the man turned toward her, she gave him a judo chop to the throat with the edge of her hand. He stumbled back into the room and was thrashing around the office holding his neck. He stumbled over the chair behind the desk and fell to the floor on his back.

Tina moved to stand over him.

His eyes were wide and he was trying to yell but all that came out, sounded to Tina, like, "Gaak, gaak."

The man shook his head back and forth, and stretched an arm toward Tina. He finally croaked out. "Please, no more, I'm done."

"Don't get up, you'll get hurt worse," she said.

Enders, in the rear room, cocked his head, "Wait… did you hear that? Something's going on out there."

The doctor with the syringe paused and looked at Enders.

The other man was gripping Jamie's arm, "You go see what's happening out front." Enders said. "I'll hold her."

After the man left, Enders said, "Okay, Doctor, go ahead."

The doctor took hold of one of Jamie's forearms while the other arm was being held by Enders. Carol left the couch and joined Enders to watch.

The doctor reached toward Jamie's arm with the syringe, his thumb on the plunger. The needle was an inch from Jamie's arm, when the doctor paused, with a puzzled look on his face. Jamie had a faint smile on her face.

When the doctor stopped, Enders looked curiously at him and saw veins pop out on the doctor's forehead, his eyeballs were bulging and sweat started running down his face.

"What's wrong Doc? Go ahead, give her the shot." Enders said.

The hand with the syringe started to shake and the doctor began a low keening moan. Jamie was calmly staring at him. The doctor let go of her arm and let out a cry of anguish. He reached over and jabbed the hypodermic needle into Enders' arm, shoved the plunger down and fell onto the floor.

Thirty Eight

"What the hell," Enders yelled, releasing Jamie's other arm. Enders, with a shocked expression, looked down at the syringe hanging from his arm. He pulled it out, flung it across the room. Then he staggered over and collapsed on the floor near the wall. He sat staring ahead with glazed eyes, breathing heavily.

Carol stumbled back in horror, not understanding what had just happened. Jamie smiled at her, "You should go back to the couch, Carol. I want you to sit down for a while."

Just then Tina and the driver tumbled through the door into the room. He was swinging at her and she was deflecting his blows and trying to kick him. He put his head down, tackled her around the waist and they fell to the floor with him on top. He made a fist and cocked his arm to punch her in the face when Jamie yelled, "Stop."

Who the hell is she? Enders wondered, in a daze, looking at Tina. The serum had made him light-headed and drowsy.

The agent was still on top of Tina with his arm back, but hadn't swung on her yet. Tina shoved him off and stood up.

Jamie told him. "Sit on the couch with Carol."

She looked at Enders, "You better get over there too." Enders stood, stumbled over and collapsed on the couch next to Carol.

"Tina, I'm glad to see you," Jamie said.

"I'm glad to see you too, Jamie," she answered, staring at the woman who was sitting on the couch with tears running down her face. "Where's Jake?"

"I haven't seen him." Jamie answered.

"He's somewhere in this building. I'm going to find him, and then we'll get out of here."

"I still don't know where my mother is. I think they're holding her some place."

"Your mother is safe, Jamie."

"She's safe?"

"Yes, we found her yesterday, and have her stashed at my house. I'll look for Jake and we'll be right back."

She headed down the hall opening doors.

Tina found Jake where Enders had left him, sitting in the chair with his head hanging down. She put her hand on the side of his face.

"Are you all right?" she asked.

"Yeah, I'll be okay when my head clears, help me up."

Tina helped me stand and we moved into the hall with my arm over her shoulders and her arm around my waist.

"Did you find Jamie?" I asked her.

"Yes, she's in the back with Enders and some of his crew. I told her that her mother is at my house."

"Will she be safe back there with Enders?"

"Uh, yeah Jake, I think she will be. He's in no condition to do anything."

We stopped at the sink long enough for me to splash some cold water on my face. I leaned against the sink with both hands for a few seconds and then stuck my head under the faucet, letting the water cascade over it.

I finally stood up straight, "I think I'm okay now, let's go get Jamie."

We went down the hall to the back room. When we entered I was stunned by what I saw. A woman I didn't know was sitting on the couch. She was crying and tears were streaming down her face. Enders and two

Thirty Eight

other men were all standing, facing the wall. Their arms were raised with palms flat on the wall. We looked in amazement at what we were seeing. They were smacking their foreheads onto the wall in unison. They all had blood trickling down their faces.

I looked at Tina.

She shrugged, "Don't ask."

I patted down Enders, found Tina's pistol and put it back in the holster.

Jamie was sitting on a chair. She stood, smiled and said, "What took so long? I'm ready to get out of this dump."

When they left, the man in the outer office was still on the floor. He raised both hands in a gesture of surrender. They went out the door and headed for the Jeep. Tina slid in behind the wheel for the drive back to San Pedro.

THIRTY NINE

In the drive back my mind was reeling with what I had witnessed. Every time I start thinking I've seen it all, I realize how naïve I am. There are forces at work all around us that are beyond human comprehension. Does Jamie really have ESP powers or is it a form of hypnotism or… what? I only know I wouldn't want to get her mad at me.

Speaking to no one in particular, I said, "I wonder how long they'll be smacking their heads on the wall?"

No one said a word. Tina turned and glanced briefly at Jamie in the back seat.

Finally, Jamie said, "They may have already stopped or they may do it forever."

Now what do I do? I have a big decision to make. I'm positive that Jamie is the girl kidnapped thirteen years ago. Should I report it to the police, with the result that Ann Gilchrist will be charged with the kidnapping? But then, who did she kidnap her from, since the child had no living relatives. I guess it could be argued that she was a ward of the county or state, therefore it was a crime in that respect. The other question is; would Jamie have been any better off if she had been adopted thirteen years ago or put in foster care? If Ann Gilchrist goes to prison, what will happen to Jamie? She is a minor and will be placed in foster care until she reaches majority age, probably eighteen. That would be over four years. In the meantime, the only mother she has ever known will be behind bars.

I leaned back and closed my eyes. I was still nauseous and recovering from the electric baton shocks. *I'll have to figure out what I'm going to do by the time we get to San Pedro.*

Two hours later, we were back to Tina's house. Jamie and her mother had a joyous reunion and I volunteered to drive them home.

"May I use the phone in your bedroom?" I asked Tina. "I have a few calls to make and some loose ends to tie up."

Jamie's mother, Ann, watched me leave the room. I'm sure she had accepted the fact that I knew about the abduction and that she probably would be facing the authorities soon.

"Sure, go ahead," Tina said. "I'm putting the coffee maker on."

I had made my decision regarding Jamie and her mother. I had to do what I believed was best for Jamie.

I dug through my wallet until I found the right card. I dialed and after a few moments heard an answer, "LAPD, Harbor Division."

"I need to speak to Detective Ernesto Chavez."

"Hang on, I think he's in, I'll ring his desk."

A few seconds, a couple clicks, then, "This is Chavez."

"Detective Chavez, this is Jacob Canoe."

"What's on your mind, Canoe?"

"I have information regarding several homicides."

After a brief silence, Chavez answered, "I'm listening."

"When we met in Gardena you asked who I was hired by, and I refused to answer because of confidentially for my client."

"Yeah."

"Well, my client was a two bit lawyer, named Baxter Harding."

"I know the scumbag, you gotta learn to pick them better."

"He actually picked us. I have reason to believe that he and at least one hired goon were responsible for the death of Mildred Lerch. The thug's first name is Cecil, last name unknown. Harding either was there or ordered the work. They were also possibly complicit in the death of Emma Thomas, a few months earlier in Hollywood."

"Do you have proof of this?"

"No, that's your job. If you go to Harding's residence, you'll find Harding and his wife's bodies. They were murdered by CIA agents led by an agent named George Enders. Harding owns a warehouse on Signal Hill where you will find the body of the aforementioned Cecil and another one of Harding's hired men. They were also murdered by Enders and his crew."

"Slow down, Canoe, I'm writing all this down."

I paused until he said, "Okay, got it so far, tell me how you know all this, Canoe?"

"I saw the bodies."

"What was the CIA involvement?"

"I'm not sure, but maybe they were also looking for the missing girl."

"Anything else you want to tell me?"

"Yes, Enders and some of his crew were in a warehouse in San Fernando as of two hours ago."

Thirty Nine

I gave him the address and waited until Chavez said, "Okay, go ahead, what else?"

"They will need an ambulance. If you hurry you might be able to find weapons matching the guns used to kill Harding, his wife, Cecil and the other man."

"Okay, Canoe, I hope that's it."

"Yeah, my investigation is over, I'm heading back to Kansas."

"I have to ask, Canoe, have you committed any crimes?"

"None that you can prove, but I did have to defend myself," I answered.

"Wait a minute, what about the kidnapped girl?"

"You were right, Chavez, when you told me that she'll never be found. She could be anywhere. We were all chasing the wrong girl."

After we retrieved my rental, Jamie and her mother got into the car and waited while I said goodbye to Tina. It was a strained conversation and neither of us wanted to say goodbye.

Tina knew I wasn't staying, although I was tempted, and I knew she wasn't going to drop everything and go to Kansas with me. She had her mother to take care of, I had my farm house and we both had our jobs. We vowed to stay in touch and try to spend vacations together.

On the drive back to Venice, I advised Ann and Jamie Gilchrist that maybe they should relocate, although they were probably no longer in danger. I never brought up the kidnapping, for which I'm sure Ann was grateful. I don't think Jamie was aware of her abduction from the hospital and what would be the point of telling her. If Ann went to prison, they would be separated and Jamie would be placed with strangers, also I can't imagine what might happen if Jamie thought her mother was in peril.

I returned the rental car and carried my suitcase across the street to the airport terminal. After buying my ticket, I found a pay phone and called Tom at the office.

After Beth paged him, Tom came on, "I was getting worried, I hadn't heard from you in two days."

"Things were moving fast and I couldn't get to a phone. I'm calling from the airport in L.A. and I'll be out of here in a couple hours."

"What time do I pick you up?"

"Don't bother, the plane will be landing in the middle of the night, I'll grab a cab to my place."

"Did you find the girl?"

"No, everything was a dead end. We were all chasing a ghost."

"What about Harding?"

"He's got no complaints, we'll never hear from him again."

"All right, Jake, take a day off and then come in. I've got another assignment for you."

In their Venice home, Jamie and her mother were preparing to go to bed. Ann was hugging her daughter, "I'm so happy to have you home."

"Me too, mom, you know, I've been thinking about something."

"What's that, Jamie?"

"We need a vacation."

"Where would you like to go?"

"I was thinking, Las Vegas."

"Hmm, yes, that sounds like fun, we'll talk about it in the morning."

Jamie fell asleep with a smile on her face.

FORTY

I was awake on the first leg of the trip, but fell asleep as soon as we left Dallas for Wichita.

It feels cool in the jungle clearing. I can hear a droning noise, probably insects in the trees. There is also a constant, barely discernable chattering noise, perhaps small animals. I'm looking at the bamboo cage. The door is wide open. My thought is that whoever or whatever was in the cage has escaped and is now free. I move closer to look in and see a much smaller cage inside. The small cage is identical to the larger except for size. It is sitting on the floor in the center of the big cage and its door is closed. I drop to a knee for a better look and then I see movement in the small cage. There is a pair of eyes looking back at me, but I can't make out the creature itself. Two small hands are pressed against the front of the cage and I watch as fingers come through the gaps and wrap around the bamboo bars. I hear a small voice and bend forward to better hear. The eyes are now closer and the face is taking shape.

I hear a voice, and then I hear it again, only louder. When something touches my shoulder I jolt awake.

"Sir, you'll have to buckle your seat belt, we're preparing to land in Wichita."

"Thank you, Miss," I said, strapping on the belt.

An hour later, the cab dropped me off at my house, where I went straight to bed and collapsed.

FORTY ONE

The sun blasting through my bedroom window woke me around eight the next morning. I showered, dressed and fried up some eggs. I was down to my last bite when I paused with the fork halfway to my mouth. I threw the fork down on the table and headed for the door. *I can't take it anymore,* I thought. I jumped in my car and headed for the Happy Trails trailer park.

Ignoring the speed limit, I tore up the road and pulled in the driveway thirty minutes later. I parked in front of the manager's unit and killed the engine. I started to step out, but paused long enough to stick my gun in the glove compartment and lock it.

A few curious kids had wandered over.

"Where's the little girl named Lisa," I asked them.

They all shrugged. One boy said, "She might be in trouble again."

"What kind of trouble, what do you mean?"

"They get real mad at her," another answered.

I heard a voice behind me, "Can I help you? I'm the manager."

"I'm asking about the welfare of a small girl named Lisa."

"Are you a cop?"

"No, I'm a private investigator, but I'm inquiring as a concerned citizen. Do you know the girl, Lisa?"

"Oh yeah, the poor kid, they're always screaming at her about something. They're down there in number 28, at the end. She stays with her mother. I guess it's her mother although she don't act like one. Her mother has a boyfriend that's usually drunk and yelling so loud we can hear him down here."

"Why don't you call the police on him?"

"He's big and meaner than hell. If he knew I called the cops on him, he'd come after me when he gets out. The pair of them are always drunk or doped up."

"Aren't you concerned about the girl?"

"Of course, but far as I know, her situation ain't that much different than any of these kids. I can't go sticking my nose in everybody's business, it's too damn dangerous."

"Have you seen her lately?"

He screwed up his face and rubbed his whiskery chin. "Well, now that you mention it, I haven't, but that's not unusual. Sometimes we don't see her for days and then she shows up again with the other kids. She often hangs around here until my missus gives her something to eat."

"Okay, I'm going down there and check on the girl. May I leave my car parked here?"

"Sure, but I'm warning you, watch out for that mean som'bitch, and try not to tear up the trailer too much."

Forty One

He pulled out a pack of Chesterfields and shook one out. As I headed up the driveway, he lit up and sat on his porch to watch the action. He turned and yelled inside his trailer, "Hey woman, get out here, this is going to be something to watch."

Four kids followed me to the trailer thinking the same as the manager. I went up the steps and knocked on number 28. A rheumy-eyed slattern opened the door. She was probably thirty years old but looked fifty. I gave her a quick glance at my badge and put it away just as quick. *I'm really putting my job and P.I. license on the line. I have no authority to do this but I really don't give a damn.*

I stepped into the trailer before she could say anything. "I'm checking on the welfare of the girl, Lisa, where is she?"

I looked around and saw the place was a filthy mess. A half dozen empty beer bottles were on a coffee table along with a full ash tray. A partially eaten slice of pizza lying on a paper plate was on a lamp table. There was an old couch with exposed springs sitting along the end wall. Next to the couch was a sweat stained stuffed chair. The worn rug was littered with cigarette burns. The kitchen counter as well as the sink was full of dirty dishes. Roaches were fearless, running around on the counter and kitchen floor. A plastic waste basket had overflowed with trash and garbage. On top of all that was a combination of odors that made me gag.

I was keeping my eye on a shivering dog lying under the kitchen table. I determined it was not going to attack me.

"Get out, she's my daughter," she yelled. "You have no business here, she's okay."

"I want to see her and talk to her, get her out here now." I said.

Tears started running down her cheeks and she was blubbering.

"No, she's my daughter and you can't see her."

She started hammering on my chest so I grabbed her wrists.

"Lisa," I yelled, "Where are you?"

I thought I heard noise, and then a weak voice, "I'm here."

The woman moved over in front of a pantry or broom closet door.

She flattened her back against the door and spread her arms to keep me out.

"Where's your boyfriend?"

"It's not his fault. She won't behave and keeps wetting her bed. He's only trying to train her."

"Move out of my way. I'm going to open that door."

"No, you can't. Pete, help me, get out here Pete," she screamed.

I heard a door open from the rear of the trailer. A big hairy pot-bellied man wearing nothing but boxer shorts was standing in the doorway.

"What the hell's going on?" he demanded.

"You must be Pete," I said.

"He won't leave, he wants to see Lisa," the woman moaned.

"Yeah, I want to see her now." I said.

He let out a loud bear like growl and charged at me with his hands in the air. He stopped about six feet from me with a surprised look when I didn't back up or run out the door.

I could tell that he was used to intimidating people with his size.

"You can't win, Pete, you're only going to get hurt. Give up the child now."

He surprised me by running at me like a football lineman, bowling me over backward on the coffee table. The table collapsed as if it was a movie prop. Bottles and cigarette butts scattered on the floor. He was hammering wildly at my face with fists the size of ham hocks. He connected a couple times and I spat blood. One or more of my teeth had cut the inside of my lower lip.

He probably out-weighed me by a hundred pounds and was sweating so much I couldn't get a grip anywhere. I was flailing around when my hand touched one of the many beer bottles strewn on the floor. I finally got a grip on the bottle neck, raised my arm and smashed the bottle on the side of his head. The bottle didn't break, but made a loud hollow "Bonk" noise. I was able to shove him to one side and slide out from under him. Another ten seconds and I may have puked from the odor of his foul breath panting in my face. I stood and headed for the cabinet door where Lisa was.

Out of the corner of my eye I watched the dog run out and take the opportunity to bite Pete on the ankle as he lay there. *Lisa isn't the only one being abused.*

As I opened the door, the woman leaped on my back and started clawing at me. With no hesitation or looking back, and without any compunction, I smacked her face with my elbow and she fell off. She was flopping around on the floor with blood running from her nose.

"She was a bad girl, we were only disciplining her. Pete didn't mean to hurt her," the woman yelled at me.

When I opened the door, I was shocked to see her purple bruised cheek and left eye almost swollen shut. Her legs were also bruised and stippled with pin points of blood from a beating with a belt or razor strap. She was sitting on a stained folded blanket and a bowl of water was on the floor next to her. She stretched her arms up to me.

Pete stood and stumbled around to maintain his balance. I'm glad I didn't have my gun. I may have killed him on the spot. I lifted my foot and kicked him in the gut as hard as I could. He stumbled back and fell out the screen door, crashing through the porch railing onto the ground. I heard a cheer go up outside from a dozen bystanders, both kids and adults.

I was sickened when the woman ran out and was sobbing over him. She was more concerned for him than she was for her daughter.

I picked up Lisa and her arms were tight around my neck. I carried her to the manager's place.

"Call the police and tell them to send a patrol car and an ambulance for this girl. She needs medical attention."

When the police arrived, I lied and told them that I was conducting an investigation nearby and heard the child crying for help. They weren't too concerned with my involvement, the abuse was obvious. They didn't hesitate in putting cuffs on the pair.

The park manager spoke to me as the cops and ambulance left. "I hope that's the last time I see those two."

"I don't know how much prison time they'll get," I answered, "But it won't be too much for what they did to the girl."

"What do you think will happen to her?"

"Probably a foster home, but she'll be better off away from her mother and that guy. I'm going to make a point to check on her from time to time." I said.

Forty One

As I climbed into my car, the dog was standing there looking at me and whining. *You look like you need a home, and maybe I could use a dog.* I got out, motioned to the dog and said, "All right, get in here."

THE END

ABOUT THE AUTHOR

Melvin Dill was born in Towanda, Kansas. Son of an itinerant oil field worker, Dill attended several different schools and graduated from Augusta High School, Augusta, Kansas. After serving on a U.S. Navy Destroyer in the Pacific, he lived in the Los Angeles area for thirty years. He now resides in Tucson, Arizona with his wife Patricia.

Printed in Great Britain
by Amazon